Superpowers in Collision

Noam Chomsky is Institute Professor at the Massachusetts Institute of Technology. He was born in Philadelphia in 1928 and educated at the Central High School, Philadelphia, and the University of Pennsylvania. He is one of the foremost figures in the field of linguistics and his book, *Syntactic Structures*, published in 1957, marked the start of a revolution in linguistic theory. He has also written widely on philosophy and political science; and his books on East–West relations include *American Power and the New Mandarins* (1969), *At War with Asia* (1970), *Peace in the Middle East?* (1974) and *Human Rights and American Foreign Policy* (1978). His latest collection of essays, *Towards a New Cold War*, appeared in 1982.

Jonathan Steele has been writing about East–West relations since the dawn of detente. After graduating from King's College, Cambridge, and spending two years at Yale, he joined the *Guardian* in Manchester. He became its East European correspondent in 1969, a job which took him on frequent visits to the Soviet Union. In 1975 he was transferred to the other pole to be the paper's Washington correspondent. As Foreign News Editor since 1979 he has continued to watch the fortunes of the superpowers, partly thanks to assignments to several hot-spots of East–West relations, such as Cuba, Angola and Afghanistan. He is the author of *Eastern Europe since Stalin* (1974) and *Socialism with a German Face* (1977), a study of East Germany, and joint author of *The South African Connection: Western Investment in Apartheid* (1973). In the British Press Awards for 1981 he was named as International Reporter of the Year.

John Gittings was born in London in 1938, is married and has four sons. He began writing on Chinese foreign policy in the early 1960s, taking issue with the general Western view of that time that China was 'bellicose' and 'expansionist'. His publications include *The Role of the Chinese Army* (1967), *Survey of the Sino–Soviet Dispute* (1968), and *The World and China 1922–1972* (1974). He has worked in Chile and Hongkong and now teaches at the Polytechnic of Central London's School of Languages, also writing regularly for the *Guardian* as its China specialist. He is a frequent visitor to China and has also built up a unique collection of Chinese popular art at the Polytechnic.

Superpowers in Collision
THE COLD WAR NOW

Noam Chomsky · Jonathan Steele · John Gittings

PENGUIN BOOKS

In memory of
Peggy Duff

Penguin Books Ltd, Harmondsworth, Middlesex, England
Penguin Books, 625 Madison Avenue, New York, New York 10022, U.S.A.
Penguin Books Australia Ltd, Ringwood, Victoria, Australia
Penguin Books Canada Ltd, 2801 John Street, Markham, Ontario, Canada L3R 1B4
Penguin Books (N.Z.) Ltd, 182–190 Wairau Road, Auckland 10, New Zealand

First published 1982

Made and printed in Great Britain by
Richard Clay (The Chaucer Press) Ltd, Bungay, Suffolk
Filmset in Monophoto Times by
Northumberland Press Ltd, Gateshead, Tyne and Wear

Contents

Editorial Note

The three talks upon which the main part of this volume is based were given at a seminar on 'The Superpowers and the Cold War' held in London in March 1981. The series was organized by Peggy Duff, General Secretary of the International Confederation for Disarmament and Peace (ICDP) – as it turned out only weeks before her death. It is to Peggy that we now dedicate our work, in memory of a splendid, tireless campaigner against injustice and for peace, who struggled to the end.

Noam Chomsky's contribution is an edited version of the transcript of his relatively informal talk to the seminar, with the addition of quotations and notes. The essays by John Gittings and Jonathan Steele are considerably expanded from the original and have been completely rewritten.

J.G.

Acknowledgements

The authors acknowledge permission to reproduce the following extracts:

from *Nineteen Eighty-Four*, reprinted by permission of the estate of the late George Orwell and Martin Secker & Warburg Ltd.

from *Present at the Creation* by Dean Acheson, reprinted by permission of Hughes Massie Ltd.

from *The White House Years* by Henry Kissinger, reprinted by permission of Michael Joseph Ltd with Weidenfeld & Nicolson.

from *Survey of International Affairs, 1947–48*, reprinted by permission of Oxford University Press.

from a JOE KRAFT column, © 1980, Los Angeles Times Syndicate, reprinted with permission.

from the *Guardian*, reprinted by permission of the *Guardian* and Harold Jackson.

from AP–Dow Jones (New York, 1 February 1980), reprinted by permission of AP–Dow Jones News Services.

The authors acknowledge the help of the seminar participants who heard the first versions of these papers, and they thank Geraldine Petley who prepared the typescript and Anna Merton who compiled the index.

Introduction:
What the Superpowers Say

John Gittings

During the 1970s we were told that we were living in the Decade of Detente and could stop worrying about the bomb while the superpowers coexisted in peaceful competition. Then, as we approached the 1980s, the authoritative voices of politicians, strategists and editorial writers began to assume a harsher tone. Detente, said one of President Carter's men, was 'a foreign word which people confuse with entente' and the President had now decided that 'peace through strength' was a better way of putting it.[1] China invaded Vietnam; the Soviet Union invaded Afghanistan; the United States refused to sign the SALT II agreement on limiting strategic nuclear weapons and made new plans for tactical nuclear war in Europe. The Chairman of the US Joint Chiefs of Staff warned that the chance of a US–Soviet military confrontation 'will increase significantly' in the first half of the 1980s.[2] The superpowers' face of benevolent despotism, promising us global stability if we behaved, was hideously distorted in the mirror of a new cold war and now threatened a horrible fate. What had we done to deserve it? Like an eclipse which the onlookers can only observe in awe, a new shadow has passed over the world. The Decade of Detente has effortlessly given way to the Dangerous Decade.

There has naturally followed an outburst of popular concern against the nuclear arms race and the threat of war, coupled with confusion and puzzlement as to why these dangers have re-emerged. But protest will not be effective unless it is underpinned by a serious political analysis of the superpower conflict which has led to the crisis of the 1980s. Nor will any popular protest movement survive some future relaxation of this crisis unless it can identify the persistent causes of conflict among the world's largest powers. (It was precisely the lack of such an analysis which led to the collapse of the anti-bomb movements of the 1960s when a new decade promised temporary detente.)

The new cold war of the 1980s is much more threatening than the old cold war of the 1950s. Not only has the size of the nuclear arsenals held by the superpowers vastly increased, but nuclear war has begun to be seen as fightable and winnable by strategists on both sides. The sheer quantity of nuclear devices, the complexity of their new technology, and the fallible sophistication of the 'early warning' methods of detection also increase the possibility of eventual use, by accident or design. But these military developments only reflect a much more significant heightening in those features of the international political scene which raise tension and increase the risks of war. The most important development has been the growth in the power of the Soviet Union relative to that of the United States. This is dangerous not because the Soviet Union is inherently more aggressive than the United States, but because – as Jonathan Steele shows here – American leaders refuse to accept the Soviet quest for 'parity' between the two superpowers. Particularly under President Reagan, although the process had already begun under his predecessor Mr Carter, the assumption (on which 'detente' was based) that Moscow and Washington could maintain a rough balance has been repudiated. Another development, arguably as important as this, has been the emergence of China as a significant force in the East–West equation. John Gittings argues in his essay that the Chinese leaders have reacted to the superpower threat in the only way they know how – by playing off one against the other. A positive relationship with both at the same time has so far been beyond their reach. This has had a disastrous effect upon the already fragile US–Soviet relationship of the early 1970s, and yet the basis for a real understanding between Washington and Peking is still very shaky.

In spite of these major developments in the past decade, the superpower struggle possesses an underlying historical logic which Noam Chomsky explores. The periodic crises of cold war are like icebergs emerging from the arctic mist; even in more normal times we still stand on shifting ice, not solid ground. The superpowers grind against each other, bruising and sometimes crushing those in their way. The cold war is not only a contest for power but a mechanism through which each maintains control over the clients and allies within its own empire. Doves and hawks alike wish to maintain that control; they only differ over the means of doing so. Their tactical assessments may vary, and they may disagree on strategy, but the goal is never questioned and in the closed world of the foreign policy establishment where they operate there is never any genuine debate over real options.

How should Britain stand in relation to the superpowers, and how should the British people view their activities? Public opinion is never encouraged to think about these questions, and we are less well informed about foreign affairs than on any other aspect of government policy. It is often said that foreign policy is 'not an issue'. It could hardly be otherwise when those who ask critical questions about it are regarded either as 'naïve' or as potential saboteurs of national security. What is the nature of the 'Soviet threat' which justifies Britain's whole diplomatic posture? In what way might the Russians practise 'nuclear blackmail' if Britain 'dropped its guard' and gave up nuclear weapons. The answers given to these questions by official spokesmen of recent Labour and Conservative governments have been rare and perfunctory, mostly showing a cynical contempt for the intelligence of the general public.

Five major debates were held in the House of Commons during 1980 and 1981 to discuss foreign and defence policy. On only one occasion did a government minister offer any sort of 'scenario' for the Soviet invasion of Western Europe against which we are supposed to keep up our guard. The speaker was Mr John Nott, Secretary of State for Defence, in the defence programme debate of 7 July 1981.

MR NOTT'S NIGHTMARE

... with a single-party state, with the Soviet leadership in the possession of overwhelming and still growing military power, who can be certain of the future? Who can tell what problems will come for its successors, with popular discontent inevitable over living standards, with demographic problems – a steep increase in the birthrate of the non-Slav peoples, especially the fifty million Muslims in central Asia – and all this held together by a repressive bureaucracy and supplied by a heavily over-centralized and inefficient economic system? Can we disregard totally even the possibility in years to come of a disintegrating Soviet empire, with, as an act of desperation, the dying giant lashing out across the central front?

(House of Commons, 7 July 1981)

Mr Nott's shooting script linked potential unrest among Tadzhiks and Uzbeks as yet unborn to a desperate decision by Soviet leaders to relieve the demographic pressure at home by launching a 'nasty and brutish' war, with Britain and West Germany as the main objectives. If it was intended as a serious scenario, the feature film to be made from it would strain credibility to the utmost. In all the defence debates in the House of Commons during 1980 and 1981 which accompanied the arguments over the decision to re-equip Britain's nuclear deterrent force with American Trident missiles, no other forecast of the circumstances under which Western Europe might be attacked was offered by any government spokesman. Nor did Mr Nott ever explain under what hypothetical circumstances the Soviet Union might use nuclear weapons 'to destroy or to blackmail us into submission'.[3] As with most British statements on the arms race, Mr Nott's vision of future war in Europe arising out of Soviet internal dissent was a straight crib from the American line of the moment. In the summer of 1981, Mr Reagan and his subordinates faced criticism from respected supporters of the policy of containment of the Soviet Union in the past, such as former Under Secretary of State George Ball and ex-ambassador Kenneth Galbraith, who now argued that Reagan's new anti-Sovietism was excessive, that Moscow had neither the influence nor the power to threaten the world and that its ideological passion had long ago been submerged by preoccupation over internal social and economic problems.[4] Quick as a flash, Mr Reagan and Mr Haig, the American Secretary of State, came back with the perfect Catch-22 rebuttal: Everything that the critics said about the Soviet problems might be true, they agreed, but the Russians only became more dangerous as they grew weaker. Mr

Lawrence S. Eagleburger, Assistant Secretary of State for European Affairs, came to Chatham House in London to read the new lesson to the British foreign policy establishment:

MR EAGLEBURGER'S ANALYSIS

On the one hand the Soviets are beset by profound problems. They are barely able to feed their people ... Spiritually they are bankrupt. As events in Poland demonstrate, the Soviet system has little attraction or relevance for others ... They have succeeded in generating the fear and hostility of every major power, from China and Japan to the United States and Western Europe ... On the other hand – and in part because of their very inability to succeed at home – the Soviets have concentrated on building a military capability well beyond any reasonable need for self-defence.

(15 June 1981)

Soviet foreign adventures, according to Mr Eagleburger, stemmed from Soviet internal weakness. But Mr Haig, in another speech, went a step further, arguing that those weaknesses were themselves a result of failures in foreign policy. Yes, said Mr Haig, the Soviet Union's 'internal problems' may lead to 'foreign diversions' – but what is the source of those internal problems? It is that 'the costs of Soviet foreign policy are growing, and no easy solutions are available' which in turn leads to Soviet consumers at home becoming 'restive'.[5] The argument had now become completely circular – and meaningless.

The same heads-I-win-tails-you-lose logic has been applied to the critical question of Soviet fossil fuel and mineral resources. If it can be shown that the Soviet Union is largely self-sufficient in these vital raw materials, that argument is then used to highlight the West's dependency upon external sources in areas which are subject to Soviet 'subversion'. If however it can be demonstrated that Moscow too suffers or will soon suffer from shortages of oil or of strategically important minerals, then it is credited with the need to expand directly into those same areas of Third World production. Mr Nott and one of his colleagues in the House of Commons have distinguished themselves by advancing both propositions to prove the Soviet threat in successive defence debates. First Mr Geoffrey Pattie, Under Secretary of State for Defence for the Royal Air Force, told the House that the Soviet Union, unlike the United States, was 'either self-sufficient or does not share the West's degree of dependence' and that this was 'likely to remain true for many years to come'. But this only made Soviet interest in the Third World a more sinister phenomenon, argued Mr Pattie, since

Soviet involvement in the developing world is therefore not a function of economic interdependence and mutual benefit. The main motive is political, and by that I mean the expansion of its influence at the expense and to the detriment of the West, Japan and China. (20 May 1981)

Six weeks later, Mr Pattie's boss said exactly the opposite when he urged the House to 'look far beyond the confines of our small corner of Europe' in contemplating the Soviet threat, and to consider the possibility that

Soviet oil production may well peak in the next two or three years, although its consumption will continue to increase. It may find new areas of production, such as the Barents Sea, and it may compensate for its lost oil export earnings by supplying natural gas to Western Europe. But Eastern Europe may be forced to buy large quantities of oil from the OPEC countries of the Middle East, with little prospect of finding the hard currency earnings to pay for it. In one area, at least, therefore – the Middle East – Soviet political, strategic and economic interest all point in the same direction. The dangers are clear. (7 July 1981)

Do the Soviet leaders offer a more convincing account of the motives behind Western foreign policy than our leaders do of theirs? The dated images of the imperialist warmonger and the arms profiteer feature prominently in their speeches, and with as little application to real circumstances, though dogma has made some concessions under the pressure of events. Since a process of detente has been initiated, it must be acknowledged that one can negotiate with some imperialists. From the years of Khrushchev (who decided that war was no longer 'inevitable') onwards, the Russians have discovered the existence of 'sober-minded' statesmen in the West who, if the wind is blowing in the right direction, are sometimes able to restrain the 'war maniacs'. This leads to

complex rationalizations when a Western leader hitherto regarded as exceptionally reactionary and warlike – Mr Nixon, for
example – becomes the instrument of detente. The whole approach
is curiously un-Marxist, with its heavy stress upon individuals,
rather than upon the social and economic forces which operate
upon them, except for the crude argument that 'militarism' is the
source of capitalism's 'super-profits'. Thus spoke Mr Brezhnev,
telling his Moscow electors that

Detente meets the interests of the peoples. The need for it is understood
by all responsible, realistic politicians. But it is opposed by strong forces
in capitalist countries that are directly or indirectly preparing a war: the
militarists, the monopolies associated with them, and their protégés in
the state apparatus and the mass media. (22 February 1980)

On Afghanistan, the weakest point in the Soviet case, Mr Brezhnev simply blustered that the United States wants 'a pretext to
extend its expansion in Asia' (although he did concede that the
US has a legitimate interest in the supply of oil from the Middle
East: 'That, in a way, we can understand').

WHAT IT'S ALL ABOUT (BREZHNEV)

Why did Washington fly into global hysterics? What is behind all
the lies about a 'Russian war against the Afghan people', the 'Soviet
threat to Pakistan and Iran', and so on? ... The wave of anti-
Soviet hysteria is being whipped up not simply for someone to win
the presidential elections this autumn on the crest of this wave. The
main motive is that the United States wants to set up a web of
military bases in the Indian Ocean, in the countries of the Near
and Middle East, and in African countries. The United States
would like to subject these countries to its hegemony and without
hindrance ship out their natural wealth. Besides, it wants to use
their territory for its strategic designs against the socialist world
and the forces of national liberation. That's what it is all about.

(22 February 1980)

As for China, Soviet leaders have no inhibitions about attribut-
ing to the Chinese expansionists the ultimate aims which, they
concede, are no longer shared by all Western imperialists – world

war and world hegemony. The modernization of China, asserts a Soviet general, 'is intended, above all, to further the Maoists' far-reaching hegemonistic goals and to support preparations for an aggressive war'.[6] The fact that the post-Mao leadership has repudiated most of Mao's policies does not weaken the Soviet analysis, which simply says that as for China's hegemonistic ambitions, nothing has changed, and that 'Having evolved from ultra-left to extreme right positions by the end of the 1970s, Chinese social chauvinism became ripe for a long partnership with imperialism and with the latter's most bellicose quarters.'[7]

While Moscow accuses Peking of social chauvinism, the Chinese have made the reverse charge of social imperialism. They too make little effort to explain how and why a country which was once their reliable socialist ally has been so transformed, except by blaming the bad guys who have taken over and become the 'New Tsars'. Stalin, in spite of his 'mistakes' (judged by Peking to occupy only 30 per cent of his total record as against a 70 per cent score of 'achievements'), was basically on the socialist track at home and abroad. When the Sino–Soviet dispute began to escalate in the early 1960s, the Chinese then decided that Khrushchev's 'revisionist clique' had taken over and was 'restoring capitalism' in the Soviet Union. Since capitalism had been restored, it followed before long that the external manifestation of Soviet policy should adopt an 'imperialist' form (since imperialism is supposed to be the monopoly stage of capitalism). By the mid-1970s great efforts were being made by Chinese ideologues to demonstrate that Soviet social imperialism met all the criteria laid down by Lenin in 1917 to define the basic features of imperialism. These included the emergence of monopolies in Soviet society, the creation of a new financial oligarchy and 'the export of capital' as an instrument of imperialism – the last proving particularly difficult since the Soviet Union invests so little abroad. Recently however this attempt to offer a theoretical basis for social imperialism has been abandoned by the Chinese, who have also become embarrassed by the previous attempts to show that capitalism was flourishing in the Soviet Union – the same arguments could too easily be turned against China's own post-Mao economic reforms. The Chinese press has now fallen back on the easier argument that the Soviet leaders are simply old-fashioned Russian expansionists, and that they have 'taken up where the old Tsars left off'.

PEKING'S DOMINO THEORY

Now the Soviet Union has clearly exposed its global strategy to dominate the world. It considers the USA to be its main enemy and Europe its main strategic target. It plans to threaten Europe via its flanks – the Middle East and Africa – and put Europe into a position where it is unable to fight. It also considers Asia and the Pacific Ocean to be an important strategic region, making moves in both the West and East. It is accelerating its expansion in other important regions and vulnerable regions of the Third World ... When circumstances require, it is ready to go to war in order to dominate the world.

(*People's Daily*, 20 May 1981)

Apart from the dire view which the superpower foes share of each other's intentions, they also have in common a disregard for historical consistency of which the Sino–US rapprochement – burying twenty years of hostile propaganda – offers the most famous example, but by no means the only one. China cannot point to any major structural changes in the Soviet state since the years of Stalin to explain why it has moved from socialism to imperialism. The Soviet Union cannot explain (without acknowledging its own major share of the blame for the Sino–Soviet split) why 'moderate' leaders, who ruled China in the 1950s and have now returned to power, should no longer seek friendship with Moscow. On the Western side, old arguments are discarded – even conceded to be incapable of proof – as they become incompatible with new justifications. Massive Western rearmament in the fifties and sixties was bolstered by loud concern that Soviet technological advances would allow Moscow to catch up and get ahead – the Sputnik scare and the missile gap. Now it is commonplace to look back, as former NATO Commander-in-Chief Alexander Haig did at a conference in 1979, with nostalgia to the time when the Soviet Union possessed 'on the strategic level ... what amounted to a 10 to 1 inferiority in 1962', and to deplore the fact that a 'rough equivalence in the US-USSR central strategic balance has now been codified' by the 1972 SALT agreement. Addressing the same conference, Mr Kissinger was even prepared to muse on the impossibility of proving that the Russians had been in need of deterrence by NATO in the past. Had deterrence been the right policy, he asked, or had 'the Soviet Union never had any intention to attack us in the first place?'

The ideological thrust behind alleged Soviet expansionism is also now widely discounted in the West. 'Trust the Communists – to be Communists' – the catch-phrase of American cold warriors in the 1950s – can be regarded by the anti-Soviet strategists of the 1980s with an indulgent smile. As another contributor to the NATO Conference put it:

... the Soviet Union will continue to develop along the lines of a traditional rather than an ideological power. Although ideology may be used under appropriate circumstances as a foreign policy tool, the Soviet view of world developments will be dictated increasingly by Russian national security interests. Similarly, Soviet instrumentalities such as military power, economic aid, and diplomacy will greatly resemble those of traditional powers.[8]

A 1980 memorandum from the British Foreign and Commonwealth Office assessing the aims of Soviet diplomacy also puts it in straightforward un-ideological terms: 'The main aim of Soviet foreign policy is to accumulate power and influence in the world as a means of preserving the security of the Soviet State.'[9] (The same might be said of the foreign policy aims of the US, China and several other powers with global pretensions, including Britain itself.) It is significant that this sort of low-key proposition is only put forward when the diplomats and strategists are talking among themselves, and is not to be found in the public speeches of Mrs Thatcher or Mr Reagan. True, any member of the public can buy the book of the NATO Conference or the proceedings of the House of Commons Foreign Affairs Committee, to whom the Foreign Office memorandum was addressed. True, anyone who reads the entire daily output of the Western press will find, buried in its thousands of pages, enough revealing stories to grasp the truth behind the propaganda. But in our complex world, most of us are not equipped to conduct the patient detective work which is required in order to penetrate the superpowers' propaganda and reconstruct the hidden historical realities of the cold war.

Yet foreign policy is far too important a business to be left to the foreign policy makers and manipulators, and today in the Dangerous Decade we all need to be historians if we are to understand and to survive. Only an informed public opinion can challenge the evasions of the superpowers and their client governments, scrutinize their actions and hold them to account for the growing threat to world peace which their policies represent. We need to puncture the bubble of respect which envelops the most tendentious and mendacious statements from 'diplomatic sources'. For the most part, what the superpowers say about one another is pure rubbish, and we should call it rubbish. The need for a critical de-mystification of cold war mythology is particularly pressing in Britain, where the Conservative government of Mrs Thatcher clings so closely to the simplistic world outlook of Mr Reagan. (As a White House spokesman exulted after her visit to the President in February 1981, 'They both know where one another has been and where one another is going. They have stared down the same gun barrel.')[10]

Stripped of the myths and the ideological self-justifications and the missionary impulse, each of the three big powers acts in terms of national security, as defined by a small group of people without public discussion. There is no surprise in this. All powers have tended to behave in this way throughout history. Britain should also act in terms of its national security, defined hopefully by a much larger group of people after wide public discussion. As a small country, Britain has little to gain from being caught up in the competition of the big powers. This book analyses how the superpower competition really works. In our conclusion we look ahead, and suggest both how the deadly triangle of superpower relations may develop, and how in broad outline a country like Britain can seek to distance itself from the struggle and to minimize its consequences.

The United States:
From Greece to El Salvador

Noam Chomsky

I would like to discuss the changes and continuities in American foreign policy since the Second World War, and then try to relate what is happening to these tendencies under the Reagan administration. There are four separate aspects of foreign policy which should be discussed at each point in time and can always be located and identified. One is the relations that are being constructed, either in fact or ideology, with the superpower enemy, i.e. with the Soviet Union and its bloc. Second, there is the set of relations that are being established with the so-called allies, the First World of the industrialist capitalist countries. Third, there are the relations with the usual victims – the Third World countries. And fourth, there is another class of victims – the domestic population of the USA. One significant feature of foreign policy is how it is constructed to deal with the problems posed by the domestic population, particularly if they are not sufficiently apathetic or obedient. As far as the continuities and changes are concerned, in the post-war period there are fundamentally no institutional changes at all. So it is reasonable to suppose – and one finds, in fact – that there is very striking uniformity of goals; that is, the fundamental conceptual apparatus remains constant for foreign policy throughout the period since the Second World War. But there are variations for a number of reasons. There are changes in individuals which often lead to change of tactical assessments as to how to achieve major goals, and of course there are objective changes in the world, which is not the same as it was in 1945.

To consider the changes in policy, it is useful to follow Michael Klare in distinguishing between 'the Prussians' and 'the Traders'. Although these groups share the same goals, the Prussians will try to attain their goals by the threat or use of force and violence while the Traders will tend to pursue them by accommodation and absorption. One could say that President Carter's National Security Adviser, Mr Brzezinski, was a Prussian, while his Secretary of State, Mr Vance, was a Trader. This is not to suggest that there is some fixity among these individuals; they can change according to their tactical assessments of the situation. Little more than tactical assessment is involved.[1]

The general framework of thinking within which American foreign policy has evolved since the Second World War is well described in the planning documents that were produced during the war by the State Department planners and representatives of the Council on Foreign Relations who met for a six-year period in the War and Peace Studies Programme, from 1939 to 1945. They knew certainly by 1942 that the war was going to end with the US in a position of enormous global dominance, and the question then arose, 'Well, how do we organize the world?' They developed the concept of Grand Area Planning, where the Grand Area is understood as that which in their terms was 'strategically necessary for world control'.[2] Their geo-political analysis attempted to determine which areas of the world would have to be 'open' – open to investment, the repatriation of profits, access to resources and so on – and dominated by the United States.

In order for the American economy to prosper without internal changes (a crucial point assumed throughout the discussions of this period), without any redistribution of income or power or modification of structures, the planners determined that the minimum area that was necessary for world control included the entire western hemisphere, the former British empire (which the US was in the process of dismantling) and the Far East. That was the minimum; the maximum was the universe, and somewhere between the two lies the Grand Area. The task was to organize it in terms of financial institutions, etc. This is the framework which remains constant throughout the whole postwar period, though one has to make adjustments when the situation changes. By and large, establishment academic scholars and journalists tend not to consider the continuities, but this is not true of the planners, who, as a ruling group, are often quite conscious of these long-term considerations. The planning documents of the 1950s in the Pentagon Papers, for example, are quite similar in tone and content to the application of Grand Area planning to south-east Asia in the 1940s, and assume the same general principles. To cite another case, illustrating the continuity of policy, Roger Fontaine, who is one of Reagan's Latin American specialists, recently made the comment that US policy towards Central America ought to be the same as it had been towards Greece in 1947.[3] That is just the right analogy to draw – more so than he may have realized. One can see very striking continuities of policy through a comparison of the two situations.

The Soviet Union played no significant role in the civil war in Greece since it recognized that this was an area central to American power. It was the first domino on the way to the Middle East – and in fact the domino theory was first formulated with explicit reference to the Greek situation. This was American turf which Stalin knew the US was not going to abandon. He was therefore trying to call off the guerrillas, much as he sought to persuade the French communists to collaborate in the re-establishment of capitalism in the early postwar years. Yet since the US was committed to using force to crush what amounted to the former anti-Nazi resistance in Greece, a justification was needed at the ideological level, and this was provided by the Soviet Union. The task was carried out quite successfully, and the success had a significant impact on the thinking of American planners. It had not been an easy task. After the war the population did not want another confrontation, but rather more refrigerators, the demobilization of the army and so on.

Top American planners were very much concerned at this situation. When the Truman Doctrine was proclaimed, Clark Clifford, one of President Truman's advisers, remarked that it was 'the opening gun in a campaign to bring people up to [the] realization that the war isn't over by any means'.[4] Truman himself told Arthur Krock, an American press pundit of the time, that he had been carrying the doctrine around with him for several months, waiting for the opportunity to use it.[5] This came when the British announced that they could no longer manage to carry off successful repression in Greece and asked the Americans to take over. There was a serious problem as to how to convince the population of the US to take on the burden. A related matter was that American planners were very much under the impact of a Depression psychology. They knew that the Depression had only ended with the war and that the New Deal measures had been essentially ineffective. Furthermore the war had created a huge industrial capacity and they were very much concerned about surplus production. This meant reconstructing European capitalism in a very specific way – by preventing it from becoming national capitalism – for the Grand Area concept will not work if various parts of the system follow their own independent course.

TRUMAN'S LEAP TO THE BOSPHORUS

... the Truman offer to Greece and Turkey, at whatever time it had been made, would have been bound to give the Soviet government a shock; for it was a fresh jump – and one of a titanic span – in the growth of an American 'hemisphere' whose expansion since the war had dwarfed the wartime expansion of Hitler's Europe and even Japan's eastern Asia ... the Russians' satisfaction at recovering gratis, as a Russian windfall from an American victory, all the assets in Chinese and North Korean territory which they had lost through their defeat in the Russo–Japanese War of 1904–5, must have been tempered by their also finding themselves faced, in consequence of the same American victory, by the United States standing on Japanese soil in the fallen Japanese Empire's shoes. And now, on 12 March 1947, the Americans had made a jump of not much shorter length and of much greater speed across the combined breadth of the Atlantic and the Mediterranean from Greenland to the Bosphorus.

(Professor Arnold Toynbee)[6]

The important task was to ensure that within the Grand Area, and particularly in industrial Europe, there would be an accommodation to American hegemony. This meant no national capitalism and certainly nothing like socialism. In addition, the system had to be rebuilt to provide opportunities for American investment and the export of surplus, which was the background for the Marshall Plan. It was necessary to create, in domestic popular consciousness, support for state policies that were costly and

ATLEE?

dangerous, involving in effect subsidies for private industry, the transfer of resources from the poor to the rich and an aggressive foreign policy. In the Third World there were many areas where force had to be used, Greece being the first one. The alleged Soviet threat – real enough in its own domains – was exploited and manipulated to mobilize popular support for these measures. The wording of the Truman Doctrine is revealing. The US was going to defend 'free people' who were threatened by 'armed minorities' or 'outside pressures'. In Greece the 'armed minorities' were the former anti-Nazi resistance which had been beaten back by Britain in its attempt to restore royalist structures, and the 'outside pressures' were to be understood as the Soviet Union. Throughout Europe the characteristic effort of the US and Britain was to try to suppress and destroy the resistance forces and restore traditional structures, which by and large meant support for fascist collaborators: in North Africa in 1942, Badoglio in Italy in 1943, and similarly in Greece where Britain invaded after the Germans had pulled out and Greece was on the road to independence. (Much the same was true in Asia, e.g. in Thailand and the Philippines.)

Truman's Assistant Secretary of State, Dean Acheson, describes in his memoirs how he succeeded in convincing congressional leaders that they should go along with the renewed war which Clark Clifford was so pleased to see breaking out again. He records a meeting in late February 1947 when congressional leaders were told that the executive needed their support for the Truman Doctrine and for subsidies to the industrial countries. The meeting went badly and no fire was lit until Acheson himself gave a speech which he describes with great pride. There was a three-pronged Russian attack with the following structure – one prong was Iran, the second was the Straits of the Dardanelles, and the third was Greece, and in all three cases the Russians were trying to take over. If the Russians broke through in any one of these places then the rot would spread to the Levant, Africa, Iran (and by implication the oil-producing zones) and south Asia, and then on to Europe, where Italy and France were threatened by the largest communist parties in the West (i.e. threatened by democratic politics).

ACHESON SEIZES HIS CHANCE

This was my crisis. For a week I had nurtured it. These congressmen had no conception of what challenged them; it was my task to bring it home. Both my superiors, equally perturbed, gave me the floor. Never have I spoken under such a pressing sense that the issue was up to me alone. No time was left for measured appraisal. In the past eighteen months, I said, Soviet pressure on the Straits, on Iran, and on northern Greece had brought the Balkans to the point where a highly possible Soviet breakthrough might open three continents to Soviet penetration. Like apples in a barrel infected by one rotten one, the corruption of Greece would infect Iran and all to the east. It would also carry infection to Africa through Asia Minor and Egypt, and to Europe through Italy and France, already threatened by the strongest domestic Communist parties in Western Europe. The Soviet Union was playing one of the greatest gambles in history at minimal cost. It did not need to win all the possibilities. Even one or two offered immense gains. We and we alone were in a position to break up the play.

(Dean Acheson, *Present at the Creation*)[7]

Acheson's success in winning over the congressional leaders is extremely important for our understanding of the structure of the cold war system. As he certainly knew, every one of those statements was a sheer fabrication. In Iran there had been a Russian attempt right after the war to support an Azerbaijani movement in the north and to gain some oil concessions, but they were quickly informed that this territory was not theirs but belonged to the West, and had withdrawn. In the Straits Stalin had made an effort to revise the Montreux Convention in his favour. Allied interchanges over this issue were convoluted. (Internationalization was regarded as a dubious solution by the US and Britain because of another sort of domino argument – if the Straits were internationalized, why not the Panama and Suez Canals?) The US fleet turned up and again by the end of 1946 this threat to peace had been contained too. And in Greece, if Acheson believed that Stalin was responsible for the guerrillas he should have fired American intelligence. Thus Acheson won over Congress by fabri-

highly possible Soviet breakthrough' and he was proud
s achievement twenty years later when he wrote his memoirs.
is is very revealing as to how the cold war was understood by
top American planners. It was a marvellous device by means of
which the domestic population could be mobilized in support of
aggressive and interventionist policies under the threat of the
superpower enemy. That is exactly the way the cold war is func-
tioning today. It is exactly the same for the Soviet Union, which
also has to mobilize its domestic population when, for example,
it invades Hungary or Afghanistan, and does so by invoking the
superpower threat: the CIA, West Germany and so on. One cannot claim that Guatemala or Czechoslovakia is a threat to either
superpower, but they become so when they are presented as out-
posts for the real enemy, with missiles and nuclear weapons and
an ample record of savagery and subversion. The cold war is a
highly functional system by which the superpowers control their
own domains. That is why it continues and will continue. It is also
a very unstable system and could blow up at any time, but planners
on both sides are willing to accept this risk for the utility of the
system in controlling their respective domains.

Immediately after the US announced, in the Truman Doctrine,
that it would devote itself to rescuing free people threatened by
armed minorities and outside pressures, an American military mission was dispatched to Greece along with substantial 'aid'. It lent
its uncompromising support to state violence, including the im-
prisonment without trial of tens of thousands of people in island
concentration camps, political executions, 're-indoctrination', the
exile of tens of thousands of Greeks, forced population removal
and similar measures. American intelligence assisted the Greek
government in carrying out mass deportations to concentration
camps and re-education centres, while forwarding to the FBI the
names of American citizens who wrote letters protesting about the
executions; the FBI reciprocated by sending reports to the American embassy on the alleged Communist ties of Greek–American
organizations. The American Chargé Karl Rankin justified
political executions on the grounds that even though political
prisoners may not, when arrested, have been 'hardened Communists, it is unlikely that they have been able to resist the

influence of Communist indoctrination organizations existing within most prisons'. He warned that 'There must ... be no leniency towards the confirmed agents of an alien and subversive influence.' These atrocities were fully supported by the US government, up to the level of the Secretary of State, George Marshall. The only worry of the American mission was that the press might report the facts.

It succeeded in preventing *The New York Times* from publishing stories on American support for repressive programmes, and in inducing the United Press to appoint a 'double-breasted Americano' as its representative in place of a *Christian Science Monitor* reporter, whom the State Department considered too leftist. The US government also succeeded in aborting an investigation of the assassination of the news correspondent George Polk when evidence began to mount that it was a right-wing assassination rather than the responsibility of the Greek left as had been claimed. Meanwhile, the USA engaged in extensive psychological warfare operations, such as fabrication of tales concerning abduction of children by guerrillas (the fabrication is conceded in internal documents), while in fact the Greek government was itself forcibly evacuating children from rebel-held territory. All of this gives the proper insight into the real meaning of the rhetoric of the Truman Doctrine, as many others throughout the world were to learn to their sorrow.[8]

Greece became an outpost for American imperial power, and was half bought out by American corporations. The way was paved for the takeover by the fascist regime in 1967 and the imprint is still there today. All of this provided a very important lesson about how to intimidate a popular movement and destroy it, how to do this within the ideological framework of an alleged Russian threat, how to bring strong forces to bear beyond the capability of an ally like the British, and how to organize Third World countries and do the job properly. The tactics and techniques proposed and used in Greece are just what one would expect to be adopted in El Salvador. In this respect Fontaine's statement noted above may be quite accurate, even if not in the sense in which he intended it to be understood.

IKE ON THE COMMUNIST MENACE

We must maintain a common world-wide defence against the menace of International Communism. And we must demonstrate and spread the blessings of liberty – to be cherished by those who enjoy these blessings, to be sought by those now denied them. This is not a new policy nor a partisan policy. This is a policy for America that began ten years ago when a Democratic President and a Republican Congress united in an historic declaration. They then declared that the independence and survival of two countries menaced by Communist aggression – Greece and Turkey – were so important to the security of America that we would give them military and economic aid.

(President Eisenhower, 21 May 1957)[9]

By 1950 this effort to rekindle international confrontation in order to solve a perceived domestic problem of over-production and the threat of depression, and the external problem of how to organize the Grand Area, had failed. As Joyce and Gabriel Kolko have shown, the Marshall Plan had some success but could by no means solve these problems.[10] It was felt that there had to be a significant revitalization of the international confrontation. It was the natural thing to do. The document called NSC 68, which was long kept secret but was finally published in 1975, was a major planning document of the early cold war, as people in the know said all along and can now be verified.[11] The principal author was Paul Nitze who is now active in the Committee on the Present Danger – one of the most hawkish lobbying groups – in April 1950, before the Korean War. It was *not* a response to the Korean War. The rhetoric of the document is semi-hysterical, a fact that is quite intriguing. Its basic line is that the cold war is a real war.

To support the war it is necessary to have a domestic national mobilization and a huge increase in the military budget. One crucial element in NSC 68 was the roll-back strategy. The attempt to absorb the Soviet Union within the Grand Area was definitely over – the Traders' response to the problem had failed. Now the Prussians took over with the idea of trying to create tensions and disturbances within the Soviet Union so that it would collapse into warring ethnic groups. The CIA was supporting guerrilla insurrections in the Soviet Union in the early 1950s at least. One can imagine the reaction if we had learned that the opposite was true in the West. Several months after NSC 68 the Korean war came along, accompanied by the same hysteria about the Russians taking over the world as in 1947, and it had the same result.

The same tactic was repeated towards the end of the Eisenhower period. In the 1960 presidential election, liberal economists supporting Kennedy (James Tobin, Walter Heller, etc.) were sharply criticizing Eisenhower because he was not sufficiently aggressive and the economy was not sufficiently geared to war. Tobin criticized Eisenhower's Defense Secretary, Charles E. Wilson, for a modest attempt to reduce the growth of military expenditure: 'At a time when the world situation cried out for accelerating and enlarging our defence effort, the administration *released* money, labour, scientific talent, materials, and plant capacity for the production of more consumer goods,' he complained.[12] The basic critique behind the slogan 'Let's get the country moving again' was that Eisenhower had not been adventuresome enough (in fact he had invaded the Lebanon, for example, but that was not very exciting).

Incidentally, some of the minor details of the Lebanon invasion give an indication of the mentality of American planners at the time, and also help to explain their feelings of outrage over their incapacity to run the world today. One can learn a good deal about these matters from the participant account by Wilbur Crane Eveland, who was then a central figure in CIA machinations in the Middle East. Eveland was ordered by CIA director Allen Dulles to go to Beirut from Istanbul when the crisis erupted, but he reports that this was difficult, because the Sixth Fleet had banned all commercial traffic from the eastern Mediterranean (Eveland was under cover, and could not go by military aircraft). Today it is unlikely that the USA could simply order all commercial traffic to be banned from the eastern Mediterranean if it decided to invade Lebanon, which offers one example of why American planners feel that they are being 'pushed around' in such an insulting way by minor powers and major enemies. American troops landed in Lebanon – in Lebanon! – with atomic-armed rockets under cover of a worldwide nuclear alert of the Strategic Air Command. When the Lebanese Commander warned that his troops might attack the American forces unless they were withdrawn, presidential envoy Robert Murphy escorted him to a window overlooking the sea and, pointing to the American carrier *Saratoga*, informed him that one of its planes could obliterate Beirut, thus ending the conversation, Eveland reports.[13]

The 'missile gap' which the Kennedy camp had exploited in order to help win the election was discovered to be a fraud as soon as it was over, but the knowledge was suppressed. Then came Secretary of Defense Robert McNamara's huge increase in the military system, setting off the big spurt in the arms race which is still going on and the growth of counter-insurgency programmes. Within the first two years of the Kennedy administration they came unpleasantly close to nuclear war three times – Cuba, Berlin and even Laos, where a mistaken report on a North Vietnamese troop offensive led to serious consideration of the use of nuclear weapons.[14]

But the Grand Area principles were severely threatened during the 1960s in a number of respects. The cost of the Vietnam war was very high and for domestic reasons Johnson was unable to declare a real national mobilization. The war was run on deficit financing, one of the causes of the relative decline of the US *vis-à-vis* its real rivals in the world – Europe and Japan. (The Soviet Union is useful as an excuse for militarization but it is not an economic competitor; its own economy barely functions.)

The USA always had an ambivalent attitude towards West European unification and the Common Market. On the one hand, given the scale of American enterprise, they were able to enter the Market and dominate competitors, but a relatively independent Europe might begin to reverse the process, which began in the 1940s, of pushing Britain and France out of their traditional domains. An independent Europe, to the extent that it unifies its currency and institutional structures, becomes a force in world affairs which is potentially on the scale of the United States or even larger. To a lesser extent the same is true of Japan; in the early 1960s the Kennedy administration was very much concerned about the viability of the Japanese economy but by 1965 the trade balance shifted in Japan's favour and with slight exceptions has stayed that way ever since. The Vietnam war became very costly to the USA and very beneficial to Japan – as had also happened with the Korean war.

By the late 1960s the situation was becoming serious. American hegemony was under serious challenge and it was obvious that something would have to be done about it. The United States now accepted what had essentially been Russian policy all along – detente as a world system of joint management, with the Russians as the junior partner. Secondly, Nixon through protectionist and neo-mercantilist measures such as import controls, suspending the convertibility of the dollar, etc., broke down the international economic system which had been constructed by Grand Area planning in the mid 1940s. This led to a domestic outcry in the United States, where those sectors of American capitalism that are concerned with international trade and investment were outraged. There were articles in the mainstream press virtually calling Nixon a criminal.[15] This was a real blow to the system within which international capitalism had been reconstructed and which produced the vast expansion of transnational corporations, and was now threatened by Nixon's neo-mercantilist measures. Nixon's efforts did not last long and were soon replaced by 'trilateralism' as the Traders came back to power.

The doctrine was put most accurately and crassly by Kissinger in his 'Year of Europe' speech of 1973: other powers have regional interests which they are to carry out within a global framework of order managed by the United States, a policy that he had also emphasized in his earlier writings. American hegemony had declined relative to that of its allies (which were really its rivals); this was a growing aspect of the international system. In his speech Kissinger referred to the danger that Europe might create a closed trading area with the Middle East and North Africa from which the United States would be excluded. This raises the continual fear of American planners that the Grand Area will break up into blocs – a dollar bloc, an ECU (European) bloc and a yen bloc – returning to a situation like that preceding the Second World War. Concern over this situation – which I believe is beginning to materialize – is one factor that lies behind the policies of the new Reagan administration.

Domestically the Vietnam war led to what is now known as the 'Vietnam syndrome', that is, the growing unwillingness of a large part of the population to support aggression and subversion. This is very serious, for it is necessary to have the population whipped into the appropriate state of chauvinist frenzy or at least beaten into apathy and obedience if there is to be the possibility of executing the Grand Area strategy at whatever level is required. Therefore a major assault had to be launched on the domestic population in the United States, side by side with the rebuilding of the basis for the assertion of American power, a revival of the pattern illustrated by the Truman Doctrine, NSC 68 and the Kennedy administration. This is what lies behind one of the most remarkable propaganda campaigns in modern history, launched in the 1970s – the 'human rights' campaign. The fact that it worked among the articulate part of the population is testimony to the amazing servility of the educated classes in the Western democracies. An extraordinary campaign was executed with great skill, selecting targets of opportunity, at a time when everyone knew beyond doubt that the United States had committed major crimes in Cuba, Indochina, Chile and elsewhere. The first step was to deflect any possible criticism of institutions; the major task of scholarship and journalism is to ensure that if bad things have happened, nobody inquires into their sources in actual institutions. It is always possible to admit that there are bad people – they can be found in the best system. Fortunately Nixon came along. He was hated anyway for other things that he had done and was marginally more crooked than other politicians, and he made the great mistake of attacking people with real power. The system rose to the opportunity. All the evil things that had been done were identified with Nixon, who was cast out of the body politic, so that it was cleansed and purified. The next act was totally predictable. A knight in shining armour came along to lead Americans on a new crusade of benevolence, the human rights crusade. Amazingly, people took it seriously. Independent journals like *Le Monde* wrote of this crusade that it was 'inconsistent' with US actions, as if the crusade were anything other than a blatantly obvious propaganda campaign to try to restore the shattered images – images which are required by any imperial power to enable it to control its own domestic population and subservient allies. Among the articulate part of the population at least it worked extraordinarily well. Arthur Schlesinger could write in the *Wall Street Journal* that the crusade was a great success and that 'In effect, human rights is replacing self-determination as the guiding value in American foreign policy.'[16] That expresses the ideological content of the propaganda system to perfection. It was taken seriously not only in the United States but also in Western Europe. The nature of this astonishing campaign was never exposed except in the most marginal circles.

By the late 1970s the Vietnam syndrome had to some extent been overcome, and in December 1978 one begins to see the expected trajectory. The date is important because this is long before the Afghan invasion and the taking of the hostages in Iran. In this month Carter made his first strong statement about increasing the military budget. The so-called 'crisis of democracy' was over and things were under control, so now a more assertive policy could be adopted to restore the international position, which had been eroded. Arms sales were increasing and it was then that the beginnings of the Reagan policy started to emerge. Sooner or later a crisis was bound to erupt that would allow the announced plans to be implemented. It was not long in coming. The taking of hostages in Iran provoked an interesting reaction in Washington: in December 1979, *The New York Times* reported an atmosphere of near euphoria in Washington with liberal senators saying that the USA had finally overcome the Vietnam syndrome, so that it could now restore the power to carry out its proper role in world affairs, while business circles also began to feel much more cheerful.

CRISES ARE GOOD BUSINESS

Foreign Policy Crises are Said to Stir Activity in US Economy. New York, 1 February 1980 (A. P. Dow Jones). At a recent luncheon meeting of business economists, Richard Everett of

Chase Manhattan Bank asked how many of the twenty-four economists present expected a recession to start during the first quarter of this year. Only three raised their hands.

That was considered a remarkable change of view in only a matter of weeks. What changed their minds was, first, the taking of US hostages by Iran and then the invasion of Afghanistan by Soviet forces. 'Khomeini and Brezhnev have postponed the recession. We're in a war economy,' declared Albert Sindlinger, an analyst whose company conducts consumer polls.

This view seemed clearly reflected in President Carter's fiscal 1981 budget that was revealed this week. The president's proposed spending will raise defence outlays 12 per cent – or 3.3 per cent when adjusted for inflation – to $142.7 billion from $127.4 billion. And outlays over the next five years are likely to be considerably higher.

(*International Herald Tribune*, 2 February 1980)

This brings us to the Reagan era. The range of policies which are now available have been well described in the current foreign policy literature, which is more authoritative than my personal interpretation would be. Consider, for example, the lead article in *Foreign Affairs* (winter 1980–81) by Robert Tucker called 'The purposes of American power'. Tucker was a Vietnam dove and is quite a respected moderate figure in international affairs; he is also the author of *The Radical Left and American Foreign Policy* – not a great book, but he was just about the only mainstream historian who took the subject seriously. The article may well be intended as a counterpart to the famous 'Mr X' article by George Kennan in 1947. It lays out the options for policy today. Detente has failed because the Soviet Union has tried to behave as an equal in international affairs. The USA now has two options, 'moderate containment' or 'resurgent America'. Tucker regards the latter as preferable if it can be achieved, but fears that the domestic world situation is such that it cannot be carried out. These options share the same assessment of what ought to be done, but differ in their tactical assessment of what the USA can get away with. Tucker distinguishes between our 'needs' and our 'wants', arguing that where needs are concerned the USA must do whatever is required. The primary need is to ensure the right of access to Middle East oil, which has been threatened not by the Russians but by indigenous elements. The USA must be prepared to use force to guarantee that right; otherwise there will be a threat to our economic welfare and to the integrity of our basic institutions. This is phraseology that could be pulled straight out of the Nazi archives. Tucker does not assume, incidentally, that Laos has a right of access to American agricultural resources, but he does assume that the USA has the right of access to the oil of the Middle East. This is a given of international affairs, and if there is a threat they have a right to use force to overcome that challenge. At this level the two options coincide.

The divergence only appears when we turn to our 'wants'. In the case of Central America, the USA 'wants' to maintain its traditional domination, but does not 'need' to. It does have the right to use military force in this area, based on two factors – tradition and pride. But the question arises as to whether it should exercise this right, and here the two options diverge. The option of moderate containment assumes that intervention will be costly and will be opposed by the domestic population and by world opinion. But if this assessment is wrong then the USA can take up the second option – that is to use force and violence to attain what it wants, and not just what it needs.

The Reagan period now marks a marginal shift from the Traders to the Prussians. Those who favour moderate containment are being displaced by those calling for a resurgent America. The handling of the Central American issue is extremely familiar, with the old record being replayed from Greece and NSC 68 and Korea onwards. The big change of policy under Reagan towards Central America is not support for the gang of murderers whom they have installed there – Carter was doing that too. Rather, it is the attempt to raise the issue to the level of an international crisis. I shall return to this crucial point, but first notice that on the issue of intervention in El Salvador too the government has succeeded in almost totally controlling the framework of discussion in the American press as of today (March 1981).

The major massacre in El Salvador – there were always smaller massacres – began in March 1980, and the State Department now claims (in the February White Paper) that from the following September a trickle of arms began to come in from Ethiopia, Cuba, Vietnam and other Russian satellites. Suppose we take the White Paper at face value: 200 tons of arms reached the guerrillas from about six months after the US-backed massacre of the peasantry began in full force – four months after the Rio Sumpul massacre, which has yet (March 1981) to be reported in *The New York Times* (in fact, even taking the White Paper at face value, what is actually reported is that some 10 tons of armaments arrived, but let us put that aside). What is the proper reaction? One possible reaction is suggested by a report by T. D. Allman in *Harper's* magazine in March 1981. Allman is one of the very few United States reporters to have taken the trouble to seek out some of the victims. He found a group of peasants who had been part of a self-help community organized by the Catholic Church, which had since been decimated by government terror. One old man told him that he had heard that somewhere across the seas there was a place called Cuba that would send them arms to defend themselves, and he asked Allman whether he could tell people in Cuba – if it really existed – about their plight, so that they could send help.

But a reaction of that sort is far from the consciousness of the American press – it is only in places like Afghanistan that it is conceivable that it might be proper to offer arms to those defending themselves from a marauding army.

EL SALVADOR: THE FACTS?

Let me take El Salvador as an example. The conclusions to be drawn from the intelligence are absolutely clear, and remain so no matter what some newspapers in the United States may claim. The Soviets, Cubans, East Germans, Nicaraguans, Vietnamese, Czechs, Bulgarians, Ethiopians and several others have been involved in the clandestine supply of arms to insurgents in El Salvador and have trained them in terrorist tactics. What they seek is a civil war, and the eventual imposition of a Marxist–Leninist dictatorship.

(US Assistant Secretary of State for European Affairs,
Lawrence S. Eagleburger, London, 15 June 1981)

US Document on Salvador Rebels 'Was Misleading'. From Harold Jackson in Washington.

The document on which the State Department relied to persuade Allied leaders to back American policy in El Salvador was yesterday described by its principal author as 'misleading' and 'over-embellished'.

Mr Jon Glassman, a State Department official who flew to San Salvador to collect and analyse captured guerrilla documents, told the *Wall Street Journal* that several reports were attributed to guerrilla leaders who had not written them and that there were mistakes and guesses by the intelligence analysts who translated the papers. 'We completely screwed it up' in identifying the guerrilla leader who was supposed to have drawn up a list of weapons arriving from various Communist countries, he said ... The 'nearly 200 tons' of military supplies said in the State Department report to have been shipped to El Salvador turns out not to have been based on the captured documents. European leaders were originally assured that 'from the documents, it is possible to reconstruct chronologically the key stages in the growth of the Communist involvement (including) the covert delivery of nearly 200 tons of arms, mostly through Cuba and Nicaragua'.

Mr Glassman has now admitted 'that comes from intelligence based on the air traffic, based on the truck traffic. In other words, it doesn't come from the documents.' The figure was calculated on the basis of a number of presumptions by the State Department analysts.

(*Guardian*, 9 June 1981)

The sole issue in the USA is whether or not the Russians sent 200 tons of arms to El Salvador. The liberals say they did but that it is not a proof of a Russian drive for global hegemony; the conservatives say they did, and that it does show that they are trying to take over the world. Meanwhile there has been literally not one article in the major American press concerning the arming of the El Salvador government forces. The impression has been conveyed that unless the USA starts to supply arms the government is going to be overwhelmed by a terrorist force with superior armaments, in which case the question arises where the weapons have come from so far. The USA has, it says, not been sending arms to the country for about three years, yet all reports indicate that there is an enormous amount of firepower at the disposal of the government forces. The latest *SIPRI Yearbook** claims that about 80 per cent of these arms came from Israel in the late 1970s. The press reports that the El Salvador government is using West German assault rifles and French helicopters and aircraft. It is clear that there is a substantial flow of arms to them, and that it has not come from the USA unless it is being diverted via Honduras. If anyone were to put the story together it might emerge that the United States has been doing on a massive scale what it has accused the Soviet Union of doing on a trivial scale – getting its various client states to send armaments to the collection of thugs who are carrying out a major massacre.

This entire topic is taboo in the United States: it cannot be discussed. Again this is a big propaganda victory. It is generally accepted that the United States is supporting a 'moderate' centrist regime, while the Soviet Union is supporting the left, and no one at all is supporting the right, and that it is the right which is responsible for terror along with the left. This is the way the problem is posed at least among those for whom the Vietnam syndrome has been overcome, including most of the intelligentsia and the political élites. It is different with regard to the general population. Here, the mood is very similar to that of 1966–7. There is substantial protest, including teach-ins and demonstrations which are barely being reported. The press learned in the late 1960s that it is a mistake to give the facts about dissenting activity. Even though the press was always hostile to the peace movement and basically pro-war, despite timid dissent over tactics, they did give some coverage to peace movement activities, which made it possible for people to understand that they were not the only ones in the world who were upset over what was going on. The peace movement was a big, chaotic, spontaneous, leaderless phenomenon. Part of what made people willing to act was the awareness that others were doing similar things elsewhere. I assume that at some point the editorial offices decided that this is not the way to handle the

* *World Armaments and Disarmament, SIPRI Yearbook 1980* (New York, Crane Russak, 1981).

problem, and as a result some quite remarkable events today are not being reported. CONSPIRACY vs COCK-UP.

For example, a group of nuns recently took over the Cambridge Office of House Minority leader Thomas (Tip) O'Neill, after he had refused to talk to a delegation that wanted to protest against government policy in El Salvador. There was no report in the press. Nothing of the sort happened during the Vietnam war, but this event was not considered newsworthy. In this case, there were, naturally, no arrests or trial. Other participants in civil disobedience are being treated much more harshly. For example, students and others in Boston who conducted a completely nonviolent sit-in at one of the registration centres in the summer of 1980 were given a thirty-day jail sentence – more than one gets for housebreaking. The Berrigan brothers and others who were on trial for damaging some missile nose-cones were not permitted to put up a political defence and may receive a very severe sentence. This is the domestic analogue to the rapid deployment force. The lesson learned by the government in Vietnam was that next time one has to come in with massive firepower and fast. That is going to be the technique at home and abroad.

The Reagan group is trying to turn the El Salvador issue into an international confrontation with the Russians in which everyone must take part. As Assistant Secretary of Defense Frank Carlucci told NATO recently, the NATO powers must help the USA bear the burden of protecting Western interests everywhere. It is very important to get Europe and Japan to line up with the United States. This can no longer be done by economic power, but it can perhaps be done under threat of military conflict.

AND PERHAPS NOT.

MR HAIG'S REAL TARGETS

The Reagan administration has deliberately raised tensions with the Soviet Union. But only partly to influence Moscow. In addition, Secretary of State Alexander M. Haig Jr sees an atmosphere of pressure as a useful background for improving the US position in many parts of the world – from China through the Middle East to Western Europe and the Caribbean ...

Whatever happens with the Soviet Union, however, Mr Haig expects a strong US line will pay dividends elsewhere. Europe, and especially West Germany, comprises his chief target ... the hope here is that a firm US stance towards Moscow will enable Mr Schmidt to dig in hard against his own left wing and reaffirm Atlantic commitments. With Bonn on board, France would be less nervous and less prone to seek insurance in Moscow ...

[As to the Middle East] He expects the Arabs will understand the need for military aid to Israel, and he even hopes that in time a fear of Moscow might draw Pakistan, Iraq and Iran towards better working relations with the United States ...

As to the Carribbean, Mr Haig is reasserting the traditional US stance as a barrier against subversion from the left. He is giving public emphasis to his support for the centre-right junta in El Salvador. By complaining of arms shipments to the revolutionaries in El Salvador, he is pointing a warning finger at the left-wing regime which replaced the Somoza dictatorship in Nicaragua, and at Fidel Castro. Mr Haig calculates that the Russians, strung out in Poland and Afghanistan, are going to back away from the Caribbean. He assumes that Mexico and Venezuela, while staying left of the United States, will cease to be outspokenly supportive of Marxist regimes in the area. He further assumes most Europeans approve self-assertion by Washington in what they regard as the backyard of the United States.

(Joseph Kraft, *International Herald Tribune*,
19 February 1981)

A major effort is now being made to compel Europe and Japan and other powers to accept a system of international confrontation in which they will be subordinated to American power. So far this has been resisted, even by Saudi Arabia, whose Foreign Minister had a special interview published in the autumn of 1980 in *Trialogue*, the journal of the Trilateral Commission, in which he said his government opposed any threat or preparation for the use of force in the Gulf region. This is not being properly reported in the press, where the impression is given that while they may say such things, the reason is that they are really frightened by the Russians. But this is a real conflict. The USA is very much concerned about the Euro-Arab dialogue and the danger that Europe will try to restore the political and economic positions from which it was excluded after the Second World War in the Middle East and Latin America. And there is a real danger that

if the Reagan administration is not successful in this effort to bring
the so-called allies into accommodation with the programme
being laid out, then it will move on to raise the level of confrontation. The USA may not be a very successful economy in
international terms any longer, but it still has enormous power.

On the domestic scene, the Reagan programme has two essential properties: first, it involves a substantial transfer payment
from the poor to the rich; second, it is a state capitalist
programme calling for a huge increase in what is in effect the
state sector of the economy, namely, military production. 'Re-
industrialization' is to be carried out by the only means possible
in a capitalist society: bribing the rich in the hope that they will
invest in industry. This is a risky proposition but it can be done
by providing a guaranteed market for high technology production
– military production. So we shall see domestic subsidies to high
technology industry through armaments. How does one sell this
programme, which means a cut-back on wages and consumption,
the production of waste and higher profits for big industry, with
a guaranteed market paid for by taxation? The only way is to have
a war, or the preparation for a war. It is an absolutely classic
pattern and, as Clark Clifford said, the population has to be convinced that 'the war is not over'. In the context of international
confrontation, they hope that the militaristic propaganda will
overwhelm the people who are suffering the blows of this programme, so that they will support the cause. The recent Chrysler
contract was the first time that a major union accepted a cut-back
in wages, and this is regarded as the opening gun in the campaign.

Internationally this will have a different effect from that of 1947.
If the United States now devotes very substantial resources to
waste production it will undermine its position in world trade.
Thus a major effort must be made to persuade Europe and Japan
to harm their own economies, through large-scale rearmament.
This is also being resisted. Significantly the resistance is coming
from Germany, which actually appears to be cutting back its
military production from 18 to 16 per cent of the budget. Japan
is also dragging its feet and is keeping its military budget at about
0.9 per cent of GNP. The USA cannot accept this, for two
reasons: first, because of international competition. One cannot

THE
NUKE
UMBRELLA

divert resources away from competitive production unless one's opponents also do so. The second reason is ideological, for if the Germans who are in the front line do not build up their military system, how does one convince Americans that they have to do so? As for the Third World, American intervention in El Salvador is really a marginal issue. They probably hope to intimidate the population without actually sending in the Marines. The real question is intervention elsewhere. While the government talks of sending a few dozen advisers to El Salvador they send 200 technicians to Oman to take part in war games. They are concerned about the possibility of intervention in an area where the USA has 'needs', and this requires a framework of assumptions that legitimates intervention.

All of these interests converge towards a policy which is designed to increase the level of international confrontation and arms production, and to create the basis and support system for intervention anywhere it is needed. The domestic population must be whipped up into a state of hysteria so that it will support the very high costs of – in a technical sense – a quasi-fascist budget. Here for once I feel moderately optimistic that they do not hold all the cards. It is very unlikely that Europe and Japan will be dragged along unless it comes to real war. The domestic scene is also much less passive than they would like to believe. With respect to El Salvador American intervention now is comparable to that in Vietnam in 1960; then one could not get two people in a room together to talk about Vietnam, but now there is a great deal of ferment and concern over El Salvador and Guatemala. The population has been substantially changed by the experience of the sixties and seventies so that these very early stages of intervention are already arousing the degree of opposition that only occurred much later on in Indochina, at a very high level of aggression. The real question now is whether people can overcome the attempt to beat the workforce and the poor into a chauvinist mood so that they will tolerate the attack being launched against them. I believe that there is a real chance of doing so, and this could have a substantial effect not only upon foreign policy but on American institutions, something that the peace movement was never able to achieve.

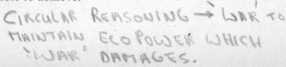

CIRCULAR REASONING → WAR TO
MAINTAIN ECO POWER WHICH
'WAR' DAMAGES.

The Soviet Union:
What Happened to Detente?

Jonathan Steele

Few people would deny that the Soviet Union and the West are launched into a new cold war. Exactly when it began and who is to blame are fiercely debated, but it is generally agreed that there was a period – now finished – in East–West relations between 1970 and 1976 which could be called an era of detente.

During that time there were four US–Soviet summit meetings, three of them on Russian soil. In 1972 Richard Nixon became the first American President to visit Moscow, fifty-five years after the Russian Revolution. His signature on an agreement limiting long-range offensive nuclear arms (SALT I) and a declaration on 'Basic Principles of Relations between the USA and the USSR' was followed over the next four years by a score of lesser treaties, covering everything from trade and grain supplies to a link-up in space of astronauts from the two countries.

In Europe the Soviet Union joined West Germany in a treaty recognizing the inviolability of each other's borders and renouncing force. It ratified a four-power agreement on Berlin, and saw its eagerly desired project for a European Security Conference come to fruition with a meeting of thirty-five heads of government in Helsinki. After the 1960s, which began with Washington and Moscow close to nuclear war over Cuba and continued with constant tension on account of Vietnam, the first half of the 1970s appeared astonishingly different. Commenting on it in March 1976, the Soviet party leader Mr Brezhnev became almost euphoric.

Soviet and American policy-makers agreed on the reasons for the change. After strenuous efforts to build up their nuclear forces, the Russians had managed to achieve a rough equivalence of armaments with the United States by 1969. Faced with a nuclear stalemate, both sides now had an interest in stabilizing the arms race. Neither of them could outgun the other, and it made little sense to try since the other side would never allow a significant gap to develop.

BREZHNEV ON DETENTE

The struggle to consolidate the principles of peaceful co-existence, to assure lasting peace, and to reduce and in the long term to eliminate the danger of world war has been and remains the main element of our policy towards the capitalist states.

Considerable progress has been achieved in the past five years. The passage from the cold war, from the explosive confrontation of two worlds, to detente was primarily connected with changes in the correlation of world forces. But much effort was required for people – especially those responsible for state policies – to become accustomed to the thought that the natural state of things is not brinkmanship but negotiation, not confrontation but peaceful cooperation ...

Though world peace is by no means guaranteed yet, we have every reason to declare that the improvement of the international climate is convincing evidence that lasting peace is not merely a good intention but an entirely realistic objective. And we can and must continue to work tirelessly to achieve it!

(Congress Report, March 1976)[1]

President Nixon's National Security Assistant, Dr Henry Kissinger, put it starkly. 'For most of the postwar period the Soviet Union had been virtually defenceless against an American first strike. Nor could it improve its position significantly by attacking since our counterblow would have posed unacceptable risks.'[2] But, starting in the middle sixties, the Russians began to augment their forces to a point where American casualties in a nuclear exchange would run into tens of millions. 'To pretend that such a prospect would not affect American readiness to resort to nuclear weapons would have been an evasion of responsibility,'[3] Dr Kissinger admitted. The United States had to accept strategic parity with the Soviet Union.

Pleased though they were to have caught up with Washington,

the Russians were not keen to be specific about their nuclear build-up. Their image as a peace-loving state, striving for disarmament, would not fit easily with admissions of a massive arms programme. Instead they used various vague formulas to describe parity. At times they talked guardedly of detente as the result of 'changes in the correlation of world forces'.[4] This was meant to imply that the main change was a general political and economic strengthening of the socialist camp in the 1960s helped by the independence of former Western colonies. At times they touched directly on their armed power, though without stressing that nuclear parity was new. 'Let no one try to talk to us in terms of ultimatums and strength. We have everything necessary — a genuine peace policy, military might and the unity of Soviet people to ensure the inviolability of our borders,'[5] Mr Brezhnev declared in 1971.

As one looks at the awesome Soviet and American military arsenals today it is easy to forget that the Russians are relative latecomers as influential world powers. The frequency of Soviet–American summits in the early 1970s as well as Moscow's public vagueness about its relatively late achievement of nuclear parity tend to foster the widespread Western impression that the world has lived for a long time under the shadow of two superpowers.

In fact this is a recent development. The Russians themselves do not admit to the description 'superpower'. They maintain that the class basis of capitalist society is entirely different from their own, and there can be no 'convergence' between socialism and capitalism. But nowadays they do admit, as the *History of Soviet Foreign Policy* puts it, to being 'one of the greatest world powers, without whose participation not a single international problem can be solved'.[6]

It is hard to exaggerate the psychological importance of parity as far as the Russians are concerned. For them detente meant that for the first time the Americans had accepted the idea of dialogue and mutually beneficial trade with the Soviet Union. This might seem a banal point but for many years the Russians had felt boycotted and ostracized by the United States. It took fifteen years after the Revolution for the United States to open diplomatic relations with the Soviet Union.

For most of the cold war the United States operated trade sanctions against the Soviet Union. To be accepted into normal international dialogue was for Moscow a major change. To be accepted as a military equal was doubly significant.

If one looks at the language of the cold war – and a study still waits to be written on the linguistic aspect of East–West relations – one finds that it is permeated with punitive overtones, the scolding attitude of a parent to a child, a judge to an accused or an animal-trainer to a savage beast. Western decision-makers talk of Moscow's 'behaviour' or 'conduct'. The Russians are frequently said to be 'on probation' or 'in the dock'.

In the early days after the Revolution the USSR was described by American Secretaries of State as 'an international outlaw'. With the collapse of detente this kind of language is gaining currency once again. The implication is that the Soviet Union is illegitimate and unworthy of being dealt with on the same level as other states. The Russian bear is part monster, part giant. President Reagan at his first press conference in the White House said the Soviet leadership reserved the right 'to commit any crime, to lie, to cheat'.[7]

REAGAN ON DETENTE

So far detente's been a one-way street which the Soviet Union has used to pursue its own aims. I know of no leader of the Soviet Union, since the Revolution and including the present leadership, that has not more than once repeated in the various Communist congresses they hold, their determination that their goal must be the promotion of world revolution and a one-world Socialist or Communist state, whichever word you want to use. Now, as long as they do that and as long as they, at the same time, have openly and publicly declared that the only morality they recognize is what will further their cause, meaning they reserve the right to commit any crime, to lie, to cheat in order to obtain it, I think that when you do business with them – even in detente – you keep that in mind.

(30 January 1981)

Dr Kissinger, writing his memoirs in 1978, described the American attitude to detente as a carrot-and-stick approach, ready 'to impose penalties for adventurism, willing to expand relations in the context of responsible behaviour'.[8] The definition of what constituted 'responsible behaviour' was clearly left to the Americans to decide.

Whether Dr Kissinger's slipping back into the inbred clichés of the cold war was conscious or not, he showed himself on occasion to be sensitive to the Soviet Union's inferiority complex, as in his comparison of his first meeting with Brezhnev with similar meetings with Mao and other Chinese leaders:

> Equality seemed to mean a great deal to Brezhnev. It would be inconceivable that Chinese leaders would ask for it, if only because in the Middle Kingdom tradition it was a great concession granted *to* the foreigner. To Brezhnev it was central. In the first fifteen minutes of our meeting, Brezhnev complained about Nixon's impromptu toast in Shanghai to the effect that the United States and China held the future of the world in their hands. Brezhnev thought this downgraded the Soviet Union, to say the least. He expressed his pleasure when in my brief opening remarks I stated the obvious: that we were approaching the summit in a spirit of equality and reciprocity. What a more secure leader might have regarded as cliché or condescension, Brezhnev treated as a welcome sign of our seriousness.[9]

Soviet leaders desperately want to feel they are part of the international community, and that they are being dealt with on a serious basis as a state with normal interests and concerns about security. They felt they were at last getting this respect out of the meetings with Kissinger and Nixon and the agreements which followed.

Detente, of course, was not just some sort of psychological therapy for the Kremlin. Washington's acceptance of the Soviet Union as a military equal offered Moscow enormous advantages. The prospect of an end to the arms race meant that there could be a 'peace dividend' for the Soviet economy. The much-neglected consumer goods and agricultural sectors could begin to get the investment they needed.

The danger of a Western invasion of the Soviet Union appeared at last to have been overcome. NATO planners may argue that theirs is a purely defensive alliance, but from Moscow it looks aggressive. For Soviet strategists, just as much as for their Western counterparts, there is no insurance as satisfying as countervailing military strength, and the Russians responded to the West's power in the traditional way by building up their own armaments. When Nixon accepted parity with Moscow, the Russians for the first time began to think that the West realized it could no longer defeat the Soviet Union in war.

Twice since the Revolution the Soviet Union has been invaded. The first time, in 1918, the attacks had come from the north and through Siberia, led by Britain and Japan. In addition, the British and French governments agreed to give secret finance to anti-Bolshevik groups in the Ukraine and the Caucasus.

As *Pravda* put it on the fortieth anniversary of the Revolution, 'the exploiting classes overthrown by the Revolution mounted a civil war against the power of the workers and peasants ... The organizer and inspirer of armed struggle against the Soviet republic was international imperialism ... Led by the leading circles of England, the USA, and France, the imperialists organized military campaigns against our country. From all sides, north, south, east and west, the attacking hordes of interventionists and White Guards poured on to our territory.'[10] Whatever exaggeration or distortion there may be in this analysis, it is part of Soviet historiography, taught in every Soviet school.

The second invasion is an issue of less international dispute. The Nazi occupation of most of the western part of the Soviet Union, the three-year siege of Leningrad, the German push to the Caucasus and the massive Soviet effort in first stemming and then reversing the Nazi onslaught cost twenty million Soviet lives. For many of the present Soviet leadership, including Leonid Brezhnev, the Great Fatherland War, as the Second World War is called, was a formative experience. After the war Stalin was determined to create a buffer zone of dependent territories in Eastern Europe. His eagerness to establish the sphere of influence tacitly conceded to him by Britain and the United States at the Yalta conference was designed to block the historic invasion route to Moscow.

Detente seemed to offer the Kremlin political as well as military reassurance. A new government in the Federal Republic of Germany was pushing an *Ostpolitik* which openly recognized the Soviet sphere of influence in Eastern Europe. The German Democratic Republic – East Germany – was finally recognized by Western states after twenty years of isolation. The Oder–Neisse line was accepted as Poland's western border. This new Western attitude of formally admitting what the Russians called 'the territorial and political realities' that resulted from the Second World War was enshrined on a continent-wide basis at the European Security Conference in Helsinki in 1975. The change in attitudes was neatly symbolized by the seating arrangements at Helsinki. They were done alphabetically, based on countries' names in French, the official language of diplomacy. Erich Honecker of East Germany found himself between Gerald Ford and Helmut Schmidt, the leaders of the two states which for twenty-five years had done more than any other to deny East Germany's existence.

Detente also gave the Russians the opportunity to step up their trade with the West, obtain Western credits and import technology. The Russians knew they were behind in certain fields and hoped to shortcut their development by buying licences or factories (so-called turn-key operations) from the West.

Finally, detente was important to Moscow as a counterweight to the West's opening to China. Faced with a hostile China on its eastern flank Russia was anxious to have a relaxation of tensions in the West. They wanted to prevent themselves being further isolated, get on an equal footing with the United States and perhaps eventually push China back into a corner.

All in all, detente provided an enormous host of benefits for the Soviet Union – military, political, economic, diplomatic and psychological. The disadvantages were on the ideological front. For some Soviet politicians brought up on a diet of implacable opposition to the West the switch to regular meetings with Western leaders and close political and commercial contacts was a shock. They feared that the change in policy would be destabilizing at home, as members of the scientific and the cultural intelligentsia began to demand an equivalent increase in international exchanges. Their fears were increased when they heard

Western politicians and the Western media explicitly demanding such changes and advocating detente as a way of 'liberalizing' the Soviet Union. Some Soviet officials were concerned that the Kremlin was giving Washington too many foreign policy concessions by restraining Soviet aid to friends and allies. The Americans admitted they wanted Moscow to rein in its support for North Vietnam in return for detente. A Politburo member, Pyotr Shelest, lost his post as the party leader in the Ukraine a few days before Nixon's first visit to Moscow because he opposed it. Other Soviet politicians felt the Kremlin had done little to help Salvador Allende, the Marxist president of Chile.

In some ways Washington and Moscow had remarkably similar views of detente. Both saw it as a device for reinforcing the status quo and pressing the other power to act predictably. Kissinger argued that if the United States could build up a web of relationships with Moscow, through trade, political dialogue and nuclear arms control, the Russians would be locked into a collaborative pattern of behaviour with the West. This would make it harder for them to break out in a wild, adventurist way. The Americans used several words which imply catching or trapping a dangerous animal. The Russians for their part saw the Americans as aggressive, bullying and trigger-happy. They hoped to modify this by accustoming Washington to regular consultation and agreement with Moscow. They talked of 'making detente irreversible', a frequent phrase in Brezhnev's speeches of the period.[11]

Detente also offered both sides costs as well as benefits. The underpinnings of each side's ideology, which was based on implacable hostility to the other (socialism versus capitalism, as Moscow saw it; freedom versus totalitarianism, as Washington saw it) were bound to be rattled when people saw their leaders chatting amicably with the enemy. The cohesiveness and internal discipline of each side's alliances in Europe were weakened, as states in Eastern and Western Europe increased their contacts without referring back to Moscow and Washington.

In spite of the similarities in each side's perception of detente, there were also major differences. Two of them ultimately caused the breakdown of detente. One was the imbalance in its ideological costs, which were greater on the American side. While the Rus-

sians had to modify their belief in the all-pervading hostility between socialism and capitalism, this was not a belief in which many
Russians took a great interest. The leadership could adjust it
without much public reaction. As for the notion that the Soviet
Union had reached parity with the United States, this was in line
with the concept of historical progress which every Russian had
been taught. It might have little operational significance, but it
was accepted as natural. Americans, by contrast, found it a far
more threatening notion. Taught that their country was the
world's most powerful nation, and 'the last, best hope of mankind', they found it hard to accept that their major ideological
enemy had become immune to attack.

The other problem was ambiguity over the area detente was
meant to cover. Was the so-called Third World affected by it?
The Russian leadership claimed to believe that it was. They hoped
the Americans would offer them a role in the Third World com-
mensurate with their status as a major nuclear power. The position
of co-chairman with Britain of the United Nations conference on
Indochina, which they had been given as long ago as 1954 (it was
revived in 1962 to deal with the Laotian crisis), was the model
they hoped to extend to US–Soviet handling of other parts of the
world. They became co-chairman with the United States of a
similar UN conference on the Middle East in 1973. At the same
time they maintained that their support for national liberation
movements in the Third World was unaffected by detente. If the
Americans continued to maintain close political, economic and
military relationships with regimes in Asia, Africa and Latin
America, they were entitled to do likewise with opposing regimes
or with guerrilla movements. Washington found this hard to
accept. It wanted to see a reduction in Soviet influence. If
Moscow wanted the benefits of nuclear detente, it must 'show
restraint' in other regions of the world. This was the essence of
the Nixon–Kissinger concept of 'linkage'. As Nixon put it in a
letter written to senior Cabinet ministers at the start of his administration:

... the previous administration took the view that when we perceive a
mutual interest on an issue with the USSR, we should pursue agreement
and attempt to insulate it as much as possible from the ups and downs

of conflicts elsewhere. This may well be sound on numerous bilateral and practical matters such as cultural or scientific exchanges. But on the crucial issues of our day ... I believe that the Soviet leaders should be brought to understand that they cannot expect to reap the benefits of cooperation in one area while seeking to take advantage of tension or confrontation elsewhere. Such a course involves the danger that the Soviets will use talks on arms as a safety valve on intransigence elsewhere ... I believe I should retain the freedom to ensure, to the extent that we have control over it, that the timing of talks with the Soviet Union on strategic weapons is optimal ... Indeed it means that we should – at least in our public position – keep open the option that there may be no talks at all.[12]

Nixon, in short, was ready to use the Russian desire for arms talks as a lever for obtaining Soviet compliance elsewhere. The difficulty was that neither side had agreed on what constituted 'compliance' or 'responsible behaviour'.

In spite of these problems the two sides maintained a dialogue on arms control until 1976, when Nixon's successor, Gerald Ford, became embroiled with Ronald Reagan in a close contest for the Republican presidential nomination. The continuing superpower dialogue was all the more remarkable since each side went on competing actively in the Third World. When President Sadat asked the Soviet advisers in Egypt to leave in 1972, the Americans promptly filled the vacuum with military aid. The United States was successful in helping to de-stabilize the Allende government, which fell to a military coup in 1973. In 1975, as Portugal's African colonies approached independence after the anti-fascist coup in Lisbon, the United States channelled money and arms to the main pro-Western guerrilla groups UNITA and FNLA in Angola – a move which the Russians subsequently matched by helping the Marxist MPLA. In South-east Asia the Russians continued to supply North Vietnam with military equipment for the final onslaught on Saigon.

By 1976 the complexities and contradictions of detente had become explosive. The fragile American consensus began to fall apart in the election campaign. The Kissinger strategy came under pressure from right-wing Republicans and from the Democrats. As the Russians saw it, there were three main factions against detente: (1) those who refused to concede parity with the Soviet Union and wanted to revert to rearmament and dealing with Moscow from 'positions of strength'; (2) those who wanted to develop a strategic alliance between Washington and China; (3) those who wanted to press for changes in the Soviet Union by forging links with dissidents and would-be émigrés. Far from resolving the debate, Carter's election victory only seemed to sharpen it. The argument over how to deal with Moscow raged publicly within the new administration. Its two wings were personified by Cyrus Vance, the detente-minded Secretary of State, and Zbigniew Brzezinski, the hawkish National Security Assistant. The President wavered from side to side.

The Russians anxiously watched the ominous signs mounting almost from the first day of the new administration. Scarcely had Carter moved into the White House when he wrote a personal letter to Andrei Sakharov, the leading Soviet dissident, and received Vladimir Bukovsky, another dissident who had just been released from a Soviet prison. The Russians saw the whole American human rights campaign as primarily directed against them and their empire in Eastern Europe. Although some members of the Carter administration made efforts to include southern Africa, the Latin American dictatorships and even South Korea for a short while, the Russians felt this was a smokescreen. They became convinced they were right, as the campaign against the Soviet Union increased, while the efforts in America's own backyard began to fade away.

Halfway through 1977 Carter took the decision to produce and deploy air-launched cruise missiles, which the Russians felt was a major escalation of the arms race. Although he also cancelled the B1 bomber, for which he was roundly criticized by lobbyists for the US Air Force, Carter argued that manned bombers were out of date and that unmanned, low-flying, cruise missiles which could evade Soviet radar made better sense.

Finally at the end of 1977 Moscow suffered a diplomatic slap in the face. The Soviet Foreign Minister Andrei Gromyko visited the United States to sign a joint statement on the Middle East, in which both sides pledged to hammer out jointly a comprehensive peace settlement. The statement caused a storm in Israel.

The Israeli Foreign Minister, Moshe Dayan, rushed to the United States and within four days the Carter administration had in effect repudiated the joint US–USSR agreement. Moscow's hopes of a revived Geneva conference and joint status with Washington were rudely dashed.

In 1978 the Carter rhetoric against the Soviet Union began to get tougher. Brzezinski visited China and tried to involve the Chinese in various actions jointly with the United States, not 'in alliance' but 'in parallel'. From the Soviet point of view this was just a semantic difference. The Russians saw the beginnings of a US–Chinese alliance aimed at them. The fruits seemed to emerge when at the point of the final discussions of the SALT II Treaty in December 1978 (which would have been accompanied by a Brezhnev visit to Washington to sign it) the Americans decided to normalize their diplomatic relations with China. It looked like a calculated snub to Moscow at best; at worst it was the decisive victory of Brzezinski in the bureaucratic struggle in Washington. The China lobby had finally defeated the arms control lobby. A further small sign of the creeping influence of China in American calculations, as Moscow saw it, was the end of the mini-thaw with Vietnam. In August 1978 the Americans had been on the verge of signing an agreement with Hanoi and then, apparently because of Chinese pressure, abandoned it. In 1979 the visit to Washington by the Chinese Vice Premier Deng Xiaoping was followed very soon by a Chinese attack on Vietnam, which the Russians believed was worked out in collusion.

On the plus side for detente the SALT summit took place in 1979, although not in one of the superpower capitals but on neutral ground in Vienna where Carter and Brezhnev signed the SALT II treaty. But Carter began to have doubts about SALT II almost before he got back to Washington. A hysterical campaign was launched against the alleged presence of a Soviet brigade in Cuba. It had been in Cuba for many years but was suddenly 'discovered' and became a lever, with the Russians being asked to 'get out of Cuba' before SALT II was ratified. This American behaviour seemed absolutely bizarre to them. The year 1979 also saw the collapse of the Shah of Iran. This activated the concept of the Rapid Deployment Force that had already been under discussion. The US Defense Secretary Harold Brown was dispatched to try to find base facilities in Kenya, Somalia and Oman for American intervention forces to cover the Indian Ocean and Persian Gulf region. Moscow interpreted this as an attempt to compensate for the American collapse in Iran and to establish some sort of American hegemony over the Persian Gulf.

At the end of 1979 NATO decided to deploy American-made cruise missiles and the advanced medium-range Pershing II missile in western Europe from 1983. The decision was described as the West's answer to Soviet deployment of a powerful new medium-range missile, the SS-20, targeted on Western Europe. The Russians argue that the new missile is only a modernized version of previous SS-4s and SS-5s, which were their answer to the British submarine-based Polaris missiles, French nuclear weapons, British Vulcan bombers, American F-111K aircraft based in Britain and other American planes with a nuclear capability based in the Mediterranean. In this tit-for-tat argument, which is symptomatic of the entire East–West arms race, the apportionment of blame is complex and ultimately unrewarding. But as the Russians saw it, the NATO decision of 1979 would give the Americans for the first time land-based nuclear missiles, many of them on West German soil, which could penetrate rapidly and irrevocably deep into Soviet territory as far as Moscow. This raised the possibility of an American first strike against the Soviet Union from Europe – a strategic nightmare which is unmatched by any equivalent threat of a forward-based Soviet attack on the United States. NATO's move came just a few months after President Carter signed a new American targeting policy known as Presidential Directive 59, which included options for a 'limited' nuclear war. American planners might, so Moscow felt, be tempted to strike first at the Soviet Union from Western Europe on the grounds that the Russians, if they counter-attacked at all, would limit their retaliation to Europe, leaving the United States immune.

American backing for detente had weakened considerably by the end of 1979. Even Kissinger, the main architect of the improvement of US–Soviet relations in the early 1970s, had shifted his position. Although the SALT II treaty signed by

President Carter was essentially the same as the draft which Kissinger had negotiated three years earlier, the former Secretary of State refused to endorse it unconditionally. At hearings before the Senate – to the dismay of the Carter administration – he listed a number of changes and assurances from the Russians which were necessary before he could support the treaty. Kissinger's retreat may have been prompted by the desire to keep in with the increasingly right-wing thrust of the Republican party, whose challenger Ronald Reagan looked a powerful opponent to Carter in the approaching election. Or Kissinger may have reflected the general ambivalence of American policy-makers towards parity. Even during the negotiations for the first SALT treaty in 1972, there were powerful groups within the Nixon administration which suspected the notion. Funds for development of the cruise missile were first included in a Pentagon budget request in the summer of 1972 only days after SALT I was initialled. The weapon clearly marked a new turn in the arms race. It had strategic potential, was not easily verifiable and could evade enemy radar. In 1973 Kissinger supported its development, mainly as a 'bargaining chip' which could be cancelled in exchange for a major Soviet concession in SALT II. Later he became convinced of its strategic advantages.

Against the background of stagnant relations with an American administration which was rearming rapidly, had apparently repudiated parity and was developing ever closer links to China, Moscow made a fateful move. In the last week of December 1979 it invaded Afghanistan.

Whether Moscow could have foreseen the international reaction to its move is hard to say. Perhaps the Russians calculated that relations with the West were already so bad that they could not become worse. Perhaps they felt the West would soon overlook it. Perhaps they thought their intervention would be short and efficient, allowing them to withdraw rapidly. Perhaps they made a mistake.

At all events their analysis of what was happening inside Afghanistan went like this. In April 1978 a national-democratic, anti-feudal coup had toppled the regime of King Daoud. The new government wanted to modernize a backward, primitive society rapidly. Unfortunately it went too far, too fast. In its impatience it managed to alienate part of the masses who should have been on its side. As internal resistance mounted, with the help of arms supplies secretly channelled to the rebels by the United States and China, the danger of counter-revolution increased. After several appeals for help from the Afghan government, the Soviet Union decided to send in about 85,000 troops. The clearest statement of Soviet actions was given by Alexander Bovin, *Izvestia*'s political correspondent, in April 1980.[13]

'WHY WE INTERVENED IN AFGHANISTAN'

The point is that the developments forced us to make a choice: we had either to bring in troops or let the Afghan revolution be defeated and the country turned into a kind of Shah's Iran. We decided to bring in the troops. It was not a simple decision to take. We weighed all the pros and cons before taking it. We knew that the victory of counter-revolution and of religious zealots and revenge-seeking feudal lords would result in a bloodbath before which even the crimes committed by the Chilean junta would pale. We knew that the victory of counter-revolution would pave the way for massive American military presence in a country which borders on the Soviet Union and that this was a challenge to our country's security. We knew that the decision to bring in troops would not be popular in the modern world even if it was absolutely legal. But we also knew that we would have ceased to be a great power if we refrained from carrying the burden of taking unpopular but necessary decisions, extraordinary decisions prompted by extraordinary circumstances...

As regards the 'non-interference' argument, I could quite simply quote appropriate clauses of the Soviet–Afghan treaty and the UN Charter. Let us get to the gist of the problem. Non-intervention is a good thing but the principles of international law do not exist in a vacuum. There was a committee for non-intervention in the affairs of Spain, and that non-intervention resulted in the forty-year dictatorship of Franco. Should the Vietnamese who were asked for help by the Khmers who were being murdered by power-crazed maniacs have read them a lecture on noninterference in reply? History and politics cannot always be fitted into legal formulas. There are situations when non-intervention is a disgrace and a betrayal. Such a situation developed in Afghanistan. And when I hear the voices of protest from people who claim to be democrats, humanists and even revolutionaries, saying they are outraged by Soviet 'intervention', I tell them this: it is logic that prompted us. If you are against Soviet military aid to revolutionary Afghanistan, then you are for the victory of counter-revolution. There is no third way.

(*Izvestia*, April 1980)

The invasion of Afghanistan produced a strong international reaction. The non-aligned nations condemned it vigorously, with more than a hundred members of the United Nations voting against the Soviet Union. In the United States and Western Europe it shook many people who had previously noted that the Russians had never before moved their troops out of the sphere of influence inherited at the end of the Second World War. It was used by hawks as a kind of *ex post facto* justification of the various moves towards rearmament and a tougher anti-Soviet stance which had been taken long before the invasion. The Carter administration ordered the CIA to coordinate a secret supply of arms to the Afghan rebels, using Chinese help. When Reagan came to power, he continued the programme, but with a different emphasis. Under Carter the aim had been to put pressure on the Russians to negotiate. Under Reagan it was meant to keep the Russians embarrassed internationally, and to prevent them from finding a solution.[14]

Reagan's tougher attitude on Afghanistan is seen in Moscow as only one symptom of a general American retreat from detente. The increasing disenchantment with detente which began under Carter has accelerated under Reagan, and will probably go on getting faster. Washington is planning the biggest increase in arms spending in American history. It is talking of supplying arms to China. It is choosing to interpret every regional conflict from Kampuchea to Angola – and even El Salvador, where Soviet involvement is minimal – as a major East–West confrontation.

The Russian response to the change in American attitudes has been remarkably consistent. Moscow continues to insist on detente. It urged the Carter administration to push for the ratification of the SALT treaty it had signed. It urged the incoming Reagan administration to reopen the dialogue on arms control. Where the Americans argue that detente has been damaged by the Soviet arms build-up the Russians say the Warsaw Pact is weaker than NATO and their global arsenal is smaller than that of the United States. Where they have superiority, in men and tanks in Europe, they justify this on the grounds that their first line of defence is based on conventional rather than nuclear weapons.

BREZHNEV ON THE ARMS RACE

We would like to hope that those who shape United States policy today will ultimately manage to see things in a more realistic light. The military and strategic equilibrium prevailing between the USSR and the USA, between the Warsaw Treaty and NATO, objectively serves to safeguard world peace. We have not sought, and do not now seek, military superiority over the other side. That is not our policy. But neither will we permit the building up of such superiority over us. Attempts of that kind and talking to us from a position of strength are absolutely futile.

Not to try and upset the existing balance and not to impose a new, still more costly and dangerous round of the arms race – that would be to display truly wise statesmanship. And for this it is really high time to throw the threadbare scarecrow of a 'Soviet threat' out of the door of serious politics.

Let's look at the true state of affairs.

Whether we take strategic nuclear arms or medium-range nuclear weapons in Europe, in both instances there is approximate parity between the sides. In respect of some weapons the West has a certain advantage, and we have an advantage in respect of others. This parity could be more stable if pertinent treaties and agreements were concluded.

There is also talk about tanks. It is true that the Soviet Union has more of them. But the NATO countries, too, have a large number. Besides, they have considerably more anti-tank weapons.

The tale of Soviet superiority in troops strength does not match the facts either. Combined with the other NATO countries, the United States has even slightly more troops than the Soviet Union and the other Warsaw Treaty countries.

So, what talk can there be of any Soviet military superiority?

A war danger does exist for the United States, as it does for all the other countries of the world. But the source of the danger is not the Soviet Union, nor any mythical Soviet superiority, but the arms race and the tension that still prevails in the world. We are prepared to combat this true, and not imaginary, danger hand in hand with the United States, with the countries of Europe, with all countries in the world. To try and outstrip each other in the arms race or to expect to win a nuclear war is dangerous madness.

It is universally recognized that in many ways the international situation depends on the policy of both the USSR and the USA. As we see it, the state of relations between them at present and the acuteness of the international problems requiring a solution necessitate a dialogue, and an active dialogue, at all levels. We are prepared to engage in this dialogue.

Experience shows that the crucial factor here is meetings at summit level. This was true yesterday, and is still true today.

The USSR wants normal relations with the USA. There is simply no other sensible way from the point of view of the interests of our two nations and of humanity as a whole.

(Twenty-sixth Party Congress, 1981)

Throughout its history the Soviet Union has felt isolated and surrounded. In seeking to safeguard the security of their territory by military stockpiling, Soviet leaders have only followed the strategy of the Tsars. As upholders of a missionary ideology which they hope will one day result in the worldwide triumph of communism they have an extra objective which the Tsars did not have. They want global influence and, in addition, as a great power, they feel they have as legitimate a right to seek influence as the United States. In practice, however, they have been cautious about trying to obtain it. Involvement in the Third World provides the Soviet Union with relatively few benefits. The Soviet Union exports no capital and earns no profits. It is almost entirely self-sufficient in raw materials and imports few essentials from the Third World. Its relationship is not that of a classic imperialism but rather a series of marriages of convenience in which Moscow mainly provides arms and technical assistance in exchange for political influence. Frequently the marriage ends in divorce, as the Russians discovered in Egypt and Somalia.

For the Kremlin the decade of the 1970s produced mixed results. It began with the American acceptance of parity and the real chance of limitations on the nuclear arms race. But it ended with an American rejection of parity and a new striving for the old supremacy. A passive, isolationist and essentially weak, albeit hostile, China turned into an actively anti-Soviet nuclear power aligned on most international issues with the West. In Afghanistan what was intended as a limited police action became a quagmire. In Eastern Europe Poland was in turmoil, raising the possibility of similar demands for political pluralism in other allied countries.

Some Western policy-makers argue that this catalogue of woes may make the next generation of Soviet leaders more hawkish than Mr Brezhnev. When the Reagan administration is not claiming that the Soviet Union is dangerous because it is strong, it is claiming it is dangerous because it is weak.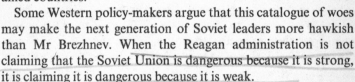

This weakness, it is said, may cause the Kremlin to 'lash out'. Others in the West cite demographic evidence for the claim that younger men will be tougher. Because the whole formative experience of Brezhnev and his colleagues was the Second World War with its cataclysmic effects on the Soviet Union, he is relatively cautious in foreign policy, it is said. (This argument is used by the same people who will also condemn the Soviet Union for being so aggressive. Somehow, in contrast to his successors, Brezhnev is suddenly transformed into a senile moderate.) Younger men who have grown up in the Cold War with no direct experience of the Second World War will be more trigger-happy.

This argument was used by Kissinger and Callaghan and is now common currency among foreign policy-makers in the West. It does not bear much examination. The generation after Brezhnev may have been too young to fight in the war, but many lost one or even two parents through it. Those really unaffected by the war will be the people born in the baby boom of the post-1945 period, who are now still only thirty-five. They will not come to power for at least another twenty years. Even for them, the argument of extra hawkishness is based on nothing more than a hunch. One could equally well argue that these people have grown up in the relative prosperity of the postwar period, have seen the standard of living grow slowly, and therefore may be more materialistic and less ideological than those who are older and lived through the sacrifices of the thirties and the war. It is also likely that the next generation of policy-makers will be more pragmatic and cautious than the Brezhnev generation because they know the wider world. After the Second World War the number of Soviet diplomats with experience of living outside their country was very small. The pool of people advising Stalin and Khrushchev was drawn from a narrow-minded group. The present group of advisers have served all over the world, not just as diplomats but as journalists (even if the latter have a very close relationship with the government) and have lived in the West and in the Third World. Talking to these people one forms the impression that they realize the limits of Soviet power much more than older Soviet people do. To itemize four areas where this is true:

1. *China*. The Soviet Union has now lived for nearly twenty years in a state of cold war with China. The Russians know that relations will not improve rapidly with China, although they hoped after Mao's death that there would be some change. For Moscow the US–China relationship has created a whole new area of instability and unpredictability in Asia. In the days when China was isolated and rhetorically extremely hawkish, the Soviet Union could outflank China from the right, arguing to countries in Asia that they, the Russians, were moderate and one had to be on guard against the Chinese in South-east Asia who were training guerrillas and trying to subvert governments everywhere. Now, as a result of the US–China link and a more forward-looking and pro-Western Chinese policy in South-east Asia, the impression has been created that it is the Soviet Union which is masterminding Vietnamese 'expansionism' while the Chinese appear moderate, thus vastly complicating Soviet relations.

2. *Islam*. This problem is as unpredictable for the Soviet Union as for the West. Neither knows how to handle resurgent Islamic nationalism. When the Shah collapsed and Khomeini came to

power, the Russians hoped to reap some rewards but they gained nothing. There is a high level of polemic between Teheran and Moscow and relations are worse now than under the Shah, when they were always correct. Relations with Libya are less close than suggested by alarmist stories in the Western media: Soviet–Libyan relations are a marriage of convenience and cannot be relied upon. Gadafy might change his mind tomorrow just as Sadat did in Egypt and Siad Barre in Somalia. Russian specialists in Moscow have no idea what will happen when Khomeini dies. There is no official line: some people say that Iran without Khomeini will be much the same; others that he may be followed by a national bourgeois regime, perhaps run by the army, which will be anti-clerical and may offer better relations.

3. *The Third World.* This is no longer predictable for Soviet policy. Under Khrushchev there was the naïve belief that because the Third World was moving away from political dependence on the West it would move into the Soviet camp. Very few countries have done so, and Russians who have served in the Third World often express disappointment and sometimes attitudes bordering on racism about their relations with Africa. The Soviet Union is also beginning to question the value of aid. In money terms it gives an enormous amount to the developing countries in weaponry and technical assistance. Of course it is concentrated heavily on key countries like Vietnam, Cuba and Ethiopia, and is not across the board. But it is a great deal of money from the point of view of the Soviet man in the street, who has to tighten his belt for it. An article in the journal *New Times* argued in veiled terms that aid is really wasted unless it goes to socialist governments who have the development interest of their country at heart. One must wait till socialism emerges in the Third World before expecting real development. Couching his argument in terms of the effect of aid upon the working class of the West, the author wrote that 'sacrifice is no way to resolve the complex problems of economic development. Anyone who propounded such belt-tightening austerity programmes would not meet with understanding in the working class and would find himself isolated'.[15] No doubt he was also talking about the Soviet working class, who are not well informed about foreign policy

and display a degree of xenophobia, which includes grumbling about aid not only to the Third World but to Eastern Europe.

4. *Eastern Europe*. The emergence of the independent trade union movement, Solidarity, during 1980 and 1981 was a dramatic reminder of the potential instability of Russia's European buffer zone. Unlike the Hungarian crisis of 1956 or the Czechoslovak one of 1968, which originated from struggles between different factions within the Communist party, the Polish upheaval was a crisis between the party and the people. Thirty-five years of Soviet-style socialism had failed to win the allegiance of vast sectors of the working class. If Poland had always been to some extent exceptional within the Eastern camp, the Russians could hardly afford to be complacent that similar disaffection might not arise, or already be latent, in Romania, Hungary, Czechoslovakia and East Germany. Martial law in Poland, though a more sophisticated technique than Soviet invasion, was neither an attractive nor a particularly effective solution. Even if political control could be restored, the economic cost of shepherding Poland out of its bankruptcy was bound to be an extra burden to the Soviet Union.

Soviet attitudes to the outside world are likely to remain cautious in the 1980s. The Russians are militarily stronger than they were in 1970, but the world beyond their borders is no more favourable to them than it was a decade ago. The United States is still economically, technologically and militarily their superior. Only in the awesome power to wreak unacceptable nuclear destruction on the other side is the Soviet Union equal to the United States. Neither side can win a nuclear war or even a nuclear arms race. That at least the Russians know. They remain committed to detente.

China:
Half a Superpower

John Gittings

On the sixth day of Hate Week ... when ... the general hatred of Eurasia had boiled up into such delirium that if the crowd could have got their hands on the 2,000 Eurasian war-criminals who were to be publicly hanged on the last day of the proceedings, they would unquestionably have torn them to pieces – at just this moment it had been announced that Oceania was not after all at war with Eurasia. Oceania was at war with Eastasia. Eurasia was an ally.

(George Orwell, *Nineteen Eighty-Four*, 1934)[1]

'The splitting up of the world into three great super-states', wrote George Orwell in his dreadful vision of 1984, 'was an event which could be and indeed was foreseen before the middle of the twentieth century.' Today we enter the 1980s in a world whose fate is already largely dominated by two and a half 'super-states' – or superpowers as they are called in a slight variation from Orwell's terminology. China is the half-superpower, but if her ambitions are satisfied, the policy of the 'Four Modernizations', proclaimed by the post-Mao leadership and including the modernization of defence, will elevate her to full superpower status before the end of the century.

An important feature of the Orwellian vision was the wholly opportunistic and shifting character of the alliances and antagonisms of the three super-states. In the real world of 1971, it was the unexpected rapprochement between Oceania (the United States) and Eastasia (China) which caught the experts napping and amazed the general public, who for the previous decade had been so firmly told that Chinese communism was an even greater threat than that of the Soviet Union. Behind Hanoi, had said President Johnson, justifying his Vietnam war, lies the shadow of Peking. Ten years later, in 1981, Secretary of State Haig would offer 'lethal' military technology to Peking with all the goodwill of a missionary offering Bibles to the converted. But Mr Haig knew – and the Chinese knew that he knew – of the tensions in the Sino–American relationship and between the ruling Chinese leadership factions which could perhaps even lead to a fresh Sino-Soviet realignment later on in the 1980s. Another feature of Orwell's world-view for 1984 sounds only too realistic today: the endemic war which never ceased between the three super-states would not, he argued, be fought out on their own territorial heartlands, but elsewhere in peripheral zones too weak to resist their depredations. Today it is indeed the peoples of El Salvador, Afghanistan and Kampuchea who suffer from the ambitions and rivalries of the superpowers – tomorrow it may be the turn of others unfortunate enough to be their neighbours.

Why did China open the door to the United States – or was it the other way around? Why did this development, which should have been so encouraging for world peace, instead make a large contribution to the instabilities of the 1980s? And why when it came to the point did the foreign policy of a self-proclaimed socialist country appear to be based so much more on national interest than on principle? The answers must be sought in the realities of international power which have faced China (and all other developing countries) over the past century and a half. For a Third World country like China, which may be geographically large but is historically weak, existing in a world dominated formerly by many great powers and more recently by two superpowers, there can be no such thing as a 'foreign policy' defined autonomously. To a very large extent the foreign policy of such a country must react to situations which are created, and to demands and threats which are made upon it, by its potential or actual enemies. Chinese foreign policy is not self-contained; even after 1949 no one was able to sit down in Peking and decide the characteristics of a 'socialist foreign policy' for China. It cannot be described in anthropomorphic terms as 'pacific' or 'bellicose', or by ascribing any other human emotion to it, as has been done by its friends and enemies. It is not often capable of taking initiatives, and it has been moulded by outside forces over a long period of time. This period can be dated back to the Opium War (1839–42) which the Chinese themselves regard as the start of their 'modern history'. China's experiences at the hands of the Western powers in this past century and more have been the dominant influence upon the formation of their view of the outside world.

This was so as much for Chinese warlords as it was for Chinese revolutionaries, but it was particularly so for Mao Zedong. The crucial role played by Mao in Chinese foreign policy consisted above all in coming to terms with the imposition of the outside world, and in working out an effective means of dealing with it. The consequences of the Chinese experience during the nineteenth century at the hands of the Western powers are such that it is hard to imagine a single act of foreign policy where China made the first move. They had to buy the diplomatic textbooks and learn the rules of the game that was already being played against them. As they became wiser they learnt how to apply the rules whenever possible to their own best advantage, and this included the lesson that it is on occasion possible to improve a weak position by playing off power A against power B. There was great jubilation when in 1899 after a string of foreign powers had obtained naval bases along the China coast, the Italians asked too and were rejected with impunity.[2] The Chinese realized that, depending on the relative weight of the adversary, it was sometimes possible to say no (unless it had the support of the other powers). During the 1910s and 1920s the Chinese position strengthened slightly as the traditional colonial powers found their attention diverted from the Far East by the First World War and its consequences. By the late 1930s the only powers which counted were the USA and Japan, with the Soviet Union as an important factor in the background.

Mao Zedong's contribution to the formation of a Chinese view of the world can be summed up in two doctrines or theories which he formulated during the revolution. First there was the theory of 'semi-colonialism'. Mao argued in the late twenties and thirties that for China to be beset simultaneously by a number of great powers put her in a stronger position than if she had been the outright colony of one power alone. It was to China's advantage to be the bone of meat for which a number of outside forces were tussling, since it became possible to play off one against the other. This was not an obvious conclusion, since many Chinese, including the first great nationalist leader Sun Yatsen, argued on the contrary that this semi-colonial status placed China in a far worse position than an outright colony like India. Mao on the other hand, both at the time and in retrospect, compared China's situation favourably with that of India, arguing that the phenomenon of 'divided rule' could be exploited by the Chinese revolution while outright colonial rule had a dampening effect upon Indian revolutionary forces. And just as the Chinese revolutionaries would play off one warlord against another and advance towards victory internally, so on a wider scale the Chinese nation could play off one foreign power against another and move towards independence externally. This view gave Mao and the Chinese communists a sense of confidence during the revolution, which persisted after 1949. When China found itself isolated internationally during the 1960s, Mao was able to remind his colleagues of this historical analogy: once again there were two dogs (the USA and the Soviet Union) tussling over the Chinese bone of meat, but because they were in contention, neither one would actually get it.[3]

The second concept, first fully grasped by Mao in the mid-1940s, was the vital importance of the Third World (or the 'colonial and semi-colonial countries' as they were then described) at a time when its revolutionary potential was not widely understood. Mao developed this view, in what became known as the 'theory of the intermediate zone', while everyone else was obsessed by the cold war in its narrow sense of the struggle between the two great blocs of the USSR and the USA. Mao argued that the real struggle was taking place not in postwar Berlin or Austria between the two dominant powers, but in the vast 'intermediate zone' of much of Asia, Africa and Latin America, where the new forces of revolutionary nationalism were fighting it out with imperialism. Mao's analysis sustained the Chinese communists during the civil war with Chiang Kai-shek at a time when they were being urged by Stalin not to rock the boat and court the risk of American intervention (which might force the reluctant Russians to take sides and thus precipitate a great-power confrontation).

Mao was able to reply that it was in the Soviet interest to approve the Chinese revolution, since his forces were taking on imperialism in the real arena, that compromise should be confined to bilateral US–Soviet relations – and that in any case he did not expect Stalin to help directly in China.[4]

These two concepts stem from the century of China's modern history – a history of dependence from which the only escape was to struggle with all the weapons available – dating from the Opium War to the Liberation. In the shorter term from 1949 onwards it has been equally true that Chinese foreign policy has not been autonomously determined, although the Chinese leaders themselves, proud of the measure of independence which was achieved, have perceived this continuing dependence less clearly. Yet Chinese diplomacy has continued to be hedged, confined and to some extent warped by the limits imposed upon it through the policies of the two superpowers. Many of the complaints levelled against China today by those on the left or in revolutionary movements elsewhere can indeed be answered by reference to this warping process and the accommodations which have been forced upon Chinese foreign policy. Domestic policy was less seriously affected, and until quite recently China's virtual exclusion from the world economic system allowed it to structure its own political economy with a fair degree of autonomy, choosing for example the system of ownership which was regarded as most appropriate for the building of socialism at a particular stage of development. But in foreign policy this was never possible. The Chinese post-1949 view of its own role in the world has been dominated almost to the exclusion of everything else by the unequal relationship between the two superpowers and China itself – now approaching the size of a half superpower, but still a long way behind.

In theory this relationship should be of a kind where China can have reasonable dealings with both superpowers at the same time. These may not be exactly equivalent, but orthodox strategic thinking would suggest that China's interests are best served if there is not an enormous imbalance in its relations with Moscow and Washington respectively. This is the same concept of a strategic balance in dealing with the other great powers which lay behind the US pursuit of detente in the early 1970s and is clearly expressed in Henry Kissinger's memoirs, where he argues that there must be some comparability in Washington's relations with both Moscow and Peking. And yet China has signally failed ever since 1949 to establish even a rough degree of comparability at the same point in time in its relations with the two superpowers, and is still unable to do so.

In 1949 the hostility between the United States and the Soviet Union had already reached the point where neither would countenance China having relations both with itself and with the other. In spite of some tentative overtures to the USA (rejected secretly by Washington except on condition that China kept its distance from the Soviet Union), China had no alternative but to choose one side and, in the famous words of Mao Zedong, 'lean to the side' of the Soviet Union. It was only in the mid-1950s that the first opportunity arose to begin to redress the balance and the Chinese were quick to seize the chance. Nothing held them back on ideological grounds. No one in Peking said that 'we cannot talk with the American imperialists because the Russians are our friends'. In essence the Chinese put forward a series of proposals to the United States – at the 'ambassadorial talks' (first in Geneva and later in Warsaw) which grew out of the 1954 Geneva conference on Indochina – which more than fifteen years later would form the basis for the eventual rapprochement of the 1970s. The formula carefully chosen in the Shanghai Communiqué of February 1972 to describe the American view on the status of Taiwan – a crucial element in the agreement – was taken word for word from a 1950s draft by an American State Department official, who was well ahead of his time (for it was never submitted to the Chinese). Mr Kissinger reflects on this fact as an oddity of history but it was not odd at all. The significance of it is clear enough: in the 1950s the Americans were not prepared to deal with the Chinese, whereas in the 1970s, for a number of good reasons (not the least being the desire to compensate for approaching defeat in Vietnam), they were.

THE TAIWAN FORMULA

Taiwan, as expected, provided the most difficult issue. We needed a formula acknowledging the unity of China, which was the one point on which Taipei and Peking agreed, without supporting the claim of either. I finally put forward the American position on Taiwan as follows: 'The United States acknowledges that all Chinese on either side of the Taiwan Straits maintain there is but one China. The United States government does not challenge that position.' I do not think anything I did or said impressed Chou [Zhou Enlai] as much as this ambiguous formula with which both sides were able to live for nearly a decade. (In fairness I must say that I adapted it from a State Department planning document for negotiations, which aborted in the Fifties.)

(Henry Kissinger)[5]

In the mid-1950s the United States had, with considerable skill, divided China from the Soviet Union, ensuring that when eventually the Chinese came to terms with the Americans this would either make Peking's relations with Moscow much worse or – as was the case – would occur against a background of an already existing rupture in the Sino–Soviet alliance. Not all American policy-makers saw this as part of a conscious strategy to split China from the Soviet Union. Some were overpowered by the same set of mystifications about the impossibility of ever talking to the aggressive Chinese with which they deluded their public. But the strategy of division was consistent in the calculations of the more sophisticated American planners. Already in 1950, behind the absurd claim that China had become a slave of Soviet imperialism and that, in Secretary of State Dean Acheson's words, the USA would have to wait till China had thrown off the yoke, lay a more sensible plan to try to detach China from this relationship.[6] By the mid-1950s, the way to do so was not – as originally proposed – to try to encourage anti-Soviet feeling in China directly. Nor was it to talk to the Chinese, who at this stage had very little to offer. It was to talk to the Russians while refusing to do so with the Chinese, who were bound to be alienated by Moscow's willingness to develop a dialogue in which they could not join. This was the dialogue which led first to a series of summits, then to the test-ban treaty and eventually to some measure of understanding on how to run the world – 'detente' – to all of which developments the Chinese took increasing exception. The Russians were also aware of the likely effect of this dynamic development upon China and from Khrushchev onwards hinted at their interest in detente as a way of 'dealing with China'. Thus they offered the weakening of their alliance with China as an incentive to the United States in order to improve their own security.[7] Both sides played a negative 'China card' in such a way as to place China in a position of acute insecurity.

By the end of 1957 the Chinese overtures to the USA had been rejected and Peking now drew the line, concluding that the balance of power would have to change before they had any prospect of meaningful negotiations with Washington. As Donald Zagoria, a CIA analyst of Sino–Soviet relations at the time, has concluded in retrospect:

To Mao, all of this must have seemed as if Khrushchev were more interested in accommodation with the United States than in supporting China. Thus, the Eisenhower policy of selective accommodation with the Soviet Union unwittingly helped to break up a Sino–Soviet alliance that had never been on very firm ground from the start.[8]

Though the US–Chinese ambassadorial talks continued sporadically, they lost their previous significance and the hard line which the Chinese now took on a variety of issues helped to earn for them the reputation of 'intransigence' which soon developed into a Western anti-Chinese dogma. It was a dangerous price to pay for preserving their own self-respect, because the labels which were now attached to Mao's government of 'xenophobia', 'irrationality' and the rest could have legitimized an attack upon China while it was still weak. Once more this willingness to take a chance illustrates Mao's unusual perception of the tactical demands of a situation. He was prepared to accept a number of years of very grave weakness while China stood on its own until the superpowers would be obliged, in his phrase, 'to take us seriously', because by that time China would have acquired the bomb and a reasonable economic potential. So during the 1960s China deliberately hemmed itself in, and although this was done for sound reasons it did encourage something of a garrison mentality. The very flexible attitude of the 1950s could not be maintained under these new conditions of isolation. The growing rigidity of Chinese propaganda strengthened the Western image of the Chinese as devil figures, an image which the Russians gladly helped to foster – the Soviet Union came out well in comparison.

By the end of the 1960s there was a convergence of conditions in which – unlike those of the 1950s – American interests would be best served by talking with China. The Peking government had acquired the strength which entitled it to be 'taken seriously'; but in so doing it had broken completely with the Soviet Union, to the advantage of the United States. By opening the door to China, the USA also hoped to get off the hook in Vietnam. If it was unable to persuade Peking to soften the terms of its defeat at the hands of the Vietnamese, it could at least win compensation by establishing a diplomatic presence in Asia where its military presence had failed. In a long-term sense the USA was still able to sabotage the Vietnamese victory, by ensuring that a united Vietnam came into existence in a situation where it no longer enjoyed the support of its closest neighbour. Just as Sino–Soviet relations had been fatally impaired by the one-sided American dialogue in the fifties and sixties, so Chinese relations with Vietnam would be finally wrecked in 1978 when Washington quite deliberately broke off discussions on economic aid to Vietnam in order to complete the 'normalization of relations' with China. (Other advantages which the opening towards China now offered to American foreign policy interests are discussed below.)

So in the early 1970s the Chinese seized the chance for which they had been patiently waiting for over two decades. They did not open the door: the door was opened to them. This interpretation does not tally with the conventional view that the Chinese became more 'moderate' and elected to 'come in out of the cold' on their own initiative. According to this view, it was the Soviet invasion of Czechoslovakia in the summer of 1968, followed by a massive build-up on the Chinese border and the serious border clashes of 1969, which prompted the first overtures from Peking. These events may have added urgency to the Chinese approach, but essentially Peking re-opened a dialogue – which they had been forced to break off ten years before – because they perceived correctly that this time the response would be positive. The first Chinese kite-flying in Washington's direction occurred as soon as Nixon was elected (in the autumn of 1968) and was accompanied by open assessment in the Chinese press of the relative weakness of the American position which would compel compromise under a new Republican president. The crude Soviet attempts to lean heavily on the Chinese – perhaps hoping to de-stabilize the Maoist forces in charge of the Cultural Revolution – no doubt added weight to the argument in favour of exploring the American path. But there is no sign of a clear strategy of Soviet pressure. The first clash on Chenpao Island had a long background of dispute; the crisis then escalated in the inexorable way of most border conflicts. The element of calculation in Soviet policy was blurred by ancient fears of the oriental hordes and the net result, which tied up over a quarter of the Soviet army's striking force on a remote Asian frontier, can hardly be regarded as a master-stroke of strategy. The most significant effect of the Soviet build-up was not to push the Chinese towards the Americans but to push the Americans towards the Chinese, since it forced Washington planners finally to discard their bipolar view of world power and contemplate the more complex pattern of triangular diplomacy. Meanwhile, to satisfy a puzzled domestic audience, the Chinese leadership justified the decision to lean towards America with a precise reference to Mao's arguments used thirty years previously in the anti-Japanese war. One had to identify the 'principal contradiction' or major enemy (Japan then and the Soviet Union now) and make common cause against it with those who posed the lesser threat (American imperialism in both cases). From this perspective an increase of perceived Soviet pressure was actually helpful to the Mao–Zhou group in helping to justify a course of action which they would in any case have wished to explore.

In February 1972 President Nixon paid his famous visit to China, met Chairman Mao, signed the Shanghai Communiqué, stood on the Great Wall, and told the assembled world press that 'This is a Great Wall.' The banality of his remark was only matched by the facile enthusiasm with which the United States government and media voiced their discovery that the Chinese were, after all, rational beings with whom one could shake hands, negotiate and exchange toasts at banquets. In downtown Peking, innocent girl shoppers were cornered by network commentators and asked, live on satellite, 'Do you date?' Trips to factories and communes, previously derided by Western scholars as worthless experiences designed only to fool the friends of China, would soon become much prized symbols of a successful 'China visit'. Not one of those scholars, nor any of the government China experts who had fed them with anti-China propaganda for the past two decades, offered a serious explanation of why the picture of an expansionist, irrational, xenophobic Peking which they had fostered for so long should now be inappropriate. The Western press generally assumed that it was the 'moderates' led by Premier Zhou Enlai who had brought China 'in out of the cold' – disregarding the clear fact that China's new diplomacy was masterminded by Chairman Mao, architect of the most immoderate Cultural Revolution (which in a less extreme form was still in progress). Others admitted that the USA had 'misunderstood' China for many years, blaming McCarthyism or the cold war or the difficulty of comprehending the Sino–Soviet dispute, but never suggesting for one moment that the misunderstanding might have masked a deliberate and successful effort to delude public opinion at home. For twenty years, wrote Dr Kissinger, US policy-makers had indeed considered China as 'a brooding, chaotic, fanatical, and alien realm difficult to comprehend and impossible to sway', and had been convinced that the Vietnam war was 'a reflection of Chinese expansionism'. But these were 'sincerely held views' which, he argued, had blinded US experts to the growing community of interest between the two countries.[9]

WHY CHINA INVITED NIXON

There are some comrades who say that, in the past, we interpreted negotiations between the US and the Soviet Union as US–Soviet collusion, but now we too are negotiating with the US. Hence, they asked whether we have changed our policy...

Our invitation to Nixon to visit China proceeds precisely from Chairman Mao's tactical thinking: 'exploiting contradictions, winning over the majority, opposing the minority, and destroying them one by one'. And this by no means indicates a change in our diplomatic line.

The two arch enemies facing us are US imperialism and Soviet revisionism. We are to fight for the overthrow of these two enemies. This has already been written into the new [1973] Party constitution. Nevertheless, are we to fight these two enemies simultaneously, using the same might? No. Are we to ally ourselves with one against the other? Definitely not. We act in the light of changes in situations, tipping the scale diversely at different times. But where is our main point of attack and how are we to exploit their contradictions? This involves a high level of tactics...

Standing at a tower overlooking the general situation of the world, having farsightedness and a correct recognition of questions, and correctly laying a firm hold on contradictions, our great leader Chairman Mao sent out all at once our ping-pong teams and invited Nixon to visit China.

(Secret Chinese foreign policy briefing, 1973)[10]

Kissinger's tactical instinct as a long-standing Realpolitiker is not completely obscured by the habit acquired later of uttering statesmanlike mystifications, and his memoirs are sufficiently revealing of the real motives behind the opening to China to merit quotation at length.

1. It would induce a 'genuine relaxation of tension' and help to establish a 'global equilibrium', but one which was based upon 'a subtle triangle of relations between Washington, Peking and Moscow' in which 'our options towards both of them [should always be] greater than their options towards each other'. (Kis-

singer disclaimed any intention of playing the 'China card', declaring that the US should 'play it straight with all parties', but this 'subtle' equilibrium was unlikely to be seen as 'balanced' by those against whom it was tilted.)

2. It would provide a lever for US pressure on the Soviet Union, although this would be routinely denied. However, messages saying that Washington had no anti-Soviet intent in its China diplomacy were not intended to be believed in Moscow. Kissinger explains: 'This is the conventional pacifier of diplomacy by which the target of a manoeuvre is given a formal reassurance intended to unnerve as much as to calm, and which would defeat its purpose if it were actually believed.'

3. Of particular importance in 1972, the China opening would put pressure on the Soviet Union to accept the US definition of detente. 'Without a China trip,' Kissinger told Nixon, 'we wouldn't have had a Moscow trip.'

4. It was designed to 'isolate(d) Hanoi diplomatically from its main sources of support'. The US would have preferred Chinese pressure on Hanoi, but 'we would be quite content with Peking's position of non-involvement'. The visit alone of an American emissary to Peking was bound to be 'traumatic'.

5. Of far deeper significance, in Kissinger's view, was the likely impact of the China opening upon public opinion in the US, which had been shocked by the Vietnam war into 'an abhorrence of foreign involvement'. It would serve instead as 'a breath of fresh air, a reminder of what America could accomplish as a world leader ... [It] would prove to ourselves and others that we remained a major factor in world affairs, able to act with boldness and skill to advance our goals and the well-being of all who relied upon us.'

6. The most seductive element in this geo-political vision for the Chinese was precisely what most alarmed the Russians – as again Kissinger candidly admits. 'With our opening to Peking the time would not be far off when all the major power centres – the United States, Western Europe, China and Japan – would be on one side and the Soviet Union on the other.'[11] This image of the world as a five-pointed star (from which the Third World was totally excluded), first expressed by Nixon in a speech while

Kissinger was visiting China, was quickly borrowed by the Chinese leaders. It satisfied both the frustrations of historical nationalism and the more recent desires for an effective anti-Soviet front.

REAGAN ON THE CHINA CARD

.. let me suggest something about the China visit that, unfortunately, the President can't say, or for that matter I can't say publicly without blowing the whole diplomatic game plan. It is true the President dressed this visit up in all the proper diplomatic, peaceful coexistence, forgive-and-forget trappings that are so much a part of the great international game. It is also true that this does confuse and disturb Republicans who have believed in his hard-headed knowledge of the Communists, if nothing else. But let's look at it as a move in a very dangerous game where the stakes are freedom itself...

American public opinion will no longer tolerate wars of the Vietnam type, because they no longer feel a threat, thanks to the liberal press, from communism, and they cannot interpret those wars as being really in the defence of freedom and our own country.

So the President, knowing of this disaffection between China and Russia, visits China, butters up the warlords and lets them be, because they have nothing to fear from us. Russia, therefore, has to keep its forty divisions on the Chinese border; hostility between the two is increased; and we buy a little time and elbow room in a plain, simple strategic move, a million miles removed from the soft appeasement of previous Democratic administrations.

(Ronald Reagan, 1972)[12]

Other Chinese leaders, less passionately anti-Soviet than Mao, saw the opening more as an opportunity for access to Western technology which had been denied during twenty years of the US-policed trade embargo. The 'modernizing' faction, led by Deng Xiaoping and with the approval of Premier Zhou Enlai, embarked in 1973-4 on their first shopping spree for Western technology – aircraft, turn-key plant, sophisticated extraction equipment, new communications technology – which set China on the track of the Four Modernizations policy, to be pursued more vigorously after Mao's death and the defeat of the 'self-reliant' faction (including the so-called Gang of Four and therefore easily discredited).

On the American side, the myth of the market of 400 million which had sustained the 'dollar diplomacy' of the early 1900s now began to assume a new reality – with twice the number of potential customers in the target area – although tinged with apprehension that other rivals would get there first. As a State Department spokesman quoted by *Newsweek* in February 1973 put it: 'If we don't recognize Peking, we encourage the Soviets to try to heal up the Sino–Soviet split and completely shut us out. And we stand in danger of seeing Japan obtain an unbeatable economic foothold.'[13] Japan, only recently denounced for a dangerous rebirth of militarism by Peking, now moved fast to regain its role as the main importer of Chinese coal, to be joined by the emerging surplus of Chinese oil. It was on this issue of the export of Chinese energy in order to pay for imports of Western technology that Deng Xiaoping and the Gang of Four finally clashed in the open political warfare of the last year of Mao's life, and the defeat of the Gang also opened the door to China's second and much more lavish spending spree of 1977–9.

THE RELUCTANT MILLIONS

William J. Casey, US Under-Secretary of State for Economic Affairs, is optimistic about opportunities for US companies in developing China's energy resources. In a speech to the National Council for US–China Trade last week Mr Casey conceded that the Chinese are reluctant to let outsiders exploit or develop their resources. But he said that he did not think they would remain 'indefinitely unreceptive' to the kind of cooperation that would enable them to sell raw materials and to benefit from advanced technology ... Mr Casey told the council, made up primarily of businessmen and bankers, that the new US liaison office in Peking will explore and assess the way the Chinese are prepared to proceed to utilize American technology and skills in their effort to develop their resources.

(Financial Times, 4 June 1973)

At the beginning of this century the US claimed to defend Chinese territorial integrity from the carve-up threatened by the other Western powers, insisting that no power should gain exclusive rights and that the principle of the Open Door should be observed. In reality, as President Wilson acknowledged later, it was 'not the open door to the rights of China, but the open door to the goods of America'. By the 1930s, the expansion of the Japanese empire threatened to close the door not only in China but throughout east Asia, leading the United States to seek economic sanctions and eventually to go to war. By the end of the Second World War one lesson more than any other had burned into the political consciousness of America's leaders: peace on American terms could only be maintained in the future if the principle of the Open Door was extended world-wide. Every nation, said Secretary of State Hull in 1943, had the obligation 'to respect the rights of others and to play its necessary part in a system of sound international economic relations'.[14] But postwar communist leadership in China closed the door, or at least ensured that the terms on which it would remain open – including the repudiation of previous treaties and debts – would be unattractive to American capital. As Chinese isolation deepened, it became a cliché of anti-China scholars to reproach the Mao leadership for its 'irrational' rejection of reliance upon what was euphemistically known as the 'international economy'. Liberal US scholars of China, arguing in favour of an end to containment, cast the same argument more positively by suggesting that if China was given access to Western technology this would encourage the growth of more 'moderate' elements in the Peking leadership. Mao Zedong, though anxious to modernize China and prepared from the start to trade on equal terms, recognized the danger of economic dependence and developed further his view of 'self-reliance' in the early 1960s. Chinese insistence on not accepting foreign credit, which struck Western economists and bankers as absurd, was explicitly based on this recognition. But Mao, on this as on other things, was not always consistent; already in 1945 he had told an American diplomat, John S. Service, that he regarded the US as 'the most suitable country to assist [the] economic development of China'.[15] In the last years of his life his approval for China's opening to the West gave the modernizing group in the leadership their own opening, although it was not until after Mao's death that the restrictions on accepting credits and loans were removed and Chinese foreign trade moved into serious deficit.

The shapers of American China foreign policy have continued to emphasize that a 'responsible' China is one whose plans for modernization are based on participation in the 'international economy' and conversely that a return to isolation would again make China a potential danger to US interests. Like the missionaries and traders who preached the Open Door eighty years ago, they see – or claim to see – United States trade with China not just as a profitable business but as a civilizing mission, even piously suggesting that it might operate both ways. As Assistant Secretary of State Richard Holbrooke argued:

Should China relapse into economic stagnation, xenophobia, or ideological frenzy borne of frustration, the consequences for world order would be profound ... More positively, we – and the world – have much to gain from a revitalized China, not only in terms of trade and economic exchange but also in terms of scientific and technological interchange.[16]

The US–China 'normalization' (i.e. establishment of full diplomatic relations) in 1979 was an overdue and inherently desirable event, but it was flawed by the motives behind it. In 1949 the US had refused to discuss diplomatic relations with the new China unless Mao's government refrained from alliance with the Soviet Union. Now China was prepared – indeed eager – to open discussions in an explicitly anti-Soviet context. In the progress towards normalization during the 1970s every gesture and move between Washington and Peking was calibrated for its effect upon Moscow, a fact which the Chinese made no effort to conceal, although the Americans formally denied it. Under Dr Kissinger in the early 1970s, the 'tilt' to China was a lever to secure Soviet compliance with the US version of detente. Under Dr Brzezinski in the late 1970s and more strikingly in 1981 when Mr Reagan offered arms to Peking, the tilt was no longer seen as an even-handed weapon between the two communist powers but a means of punishing the Soviet Union for its transgressions. In the speech quoted above in 1980 Assistant Secretary of State Richard Holbrooke formally announced the abandonment of a balanced policy, claiming that relations with China should now be pursued in their own right. But the connection, having been established by deliberate acts of American diplomacy, could not be arbitrarily severed, and there was no reason why the Soviet Union should stop interpreting US pro-China moves as directed against them, especially when they increasingly involved the offer of military-related supplies.

THE CHINESE VIEW FROM MOSCOW

From the point of view hypothetically of a Soviet strategic planner, the Soviet Union face twenty-six potential enemies, which is quite a problem ... I do not believe they have rid themselves of the notion that was developed early in the 1970s that the Soviet Union cannot be outflanked in a big, strategic sense, and that was given greater urgency when that severe shock was administered to the Soviet system in the Sino–Japanese rapprochement. I think they thought this was inconceivable and now there are possibilities of an EEC–Peking axis. They are very concerned about the potentiality of the Peking axis. The job I would not like would be to be a Soviet strategic planner for the 1980s.

Professor John Erickson[17]

One pro-China official agrued that 'to retard the development of Sino–American relations because Soviet–American relations have soured would be to punish Beijing [Peking] for Moscow's aggression' – as if the souring of one had not already been accelerated by the 'development' of the other.[18]

A real problem still existed between the US and China – that of Taiwan – delaying the completion of 'normalization' until the end of 1978. In what may prove to be a fatal weakness in the new relationship, the problem was not solved but merely shelved in the interests of the wider anti-Soviet purpose. Since the ambassadorial talks of the mid-1950s, the Taiwan question had been simple but intractable: the US demanded that China should 'renounce the use of force', or give some other clear indication that they would not attempt to regain the island by coercive means if American military support was withdrawn from it. China on the other hand demanded that such support should be withdrawn completely, and was only prepared to say that it preferred a peaceful approach to re-integration, while reserving the right to use force in what after all was its own territory. As late as the Peking visit of Secretary of State Vance in August 1977, these two positions still seemed incompatible. By now it was admitted by American advocates of 'normalization' that 'the domestic political momentum towards normalization [had] just about played itself out in both the United States and the PRC'. A fork had been reached in the road: the turning which they feared would carry the US inexorably away from detente.[19]

It was no coincidence that the momentum was resumed in spring 1978 with an explicit anti-Soviet thrust just when Soviet–American relations began to take a sharp turn for the worse. Mr Brzezinski signalled the shift. 'The American–Chinese relationship is a central element of our new global policy,' he said in April before visiting China, where he told the Chinese that 'our separate actions will be mutually supportive in many areas where we have common concern'. On his return this new view, which came close to enlisting China as an anti-Soviet ally, began cautiously to be made public; a fundamental policy decision had been made 'that China shares strategic concerns with both the United States and its allies, and that a strong and secure China serves American national interests'.[20]

On the Chinese side the growing commitment to the policy of Four Modernizations, now reaffirmed by Mr Deng Xiaoping to every foreign visitor, made the USA seem a patron worth cultivating, not just as insurance against the Russians but as a prime source of 'advanced science and technology'. American officials travelling with Mr Brzezinski reported that the Chinese had become much less 'prickly about national sovereignty' in allowing foreign conditions on the supply of technical equipment. There had been a considerable 'mellowing and relaxing' in accepting Western proposals involving technology since the death of Mao Zedong in 1976.[21] As a reward and further incentive, the

Carter administration made its first offer of 'dual-use' equipment, i.e. technology for civilian use which could also have a military application.

The normalization deal finally struck in December 1978 bore the classic mark of opportunism on a grand scale – masked by talk of 'friendship' which neither side took seriously.

Though China did not actually forswear the 'use of force' to regain Taiwan, it conceded as much indirectly. For while the US announced that it would let the US–Taiwan Military Defence Agreement expire in a year's time, it also insisted that it would continue to supply the island with 'defensive weapons'. China formally objected, but still signed. High in the administration, *The New York Times* reports, 'officials could barely contain their satisfaction with the turn of events. "We got it on our terms", one of them said' (16 Dec 1978). But Mr Deng, using his foreign policy exploits to weaken domestic criticism of the modernization policy and his rejection of the Cultural Revolution, could also claim that the deal had been profitable. In return the Carter administration allowed Mr Deng Xiaoping to use his Washington visit for crude propaganda attacks on 'the polar bear' and even to announce at a Washington press conference his intention of 'teaching Vietnam a lesson'. Within days of returning to Peking, Deng had ordered the Chinese People's Liberation Army to invade Vietnam in an offensive operation which was only perfunctorily justified by China as a 'defensive counter-attack'. The US had nothing to say, while Britain blamed the Vietnamese.[22]

These events were watched from Moscow with evident concern, reported fully by the American press and acknowledged complacently by American leaders. Mr Brezhnev, it was agreed, 'has had to accept a series of setbacks' and for the time being he could do nothing about it. Mr Carter made things worse by distorting a private message from the Soviet Premier to make it appear that he had no objection to the way in which US–China relations had been normalized. Less well noted were the warnings issued by Russian officials that they would find some way in the future of evening the score: 'We'll also have a party in our street,' they said, using a phrase which had been popular in the early days of war with Germany to indicate that the time for revenge would not be long delayed.[23]

The shaky basis of the Sino – American entente was demonstrated in June 1981 when President Reagan's Secretary of State, Alexander Haig, visited Peking with an invitation to the Chinese Defence minister to come shopping in the United States for 'lethal' weapons. In part this reflected Mr Reagan's deliberate raising of the stakes in the US–Soviet relationship as he sought to re-create the Eisenhower era of 'negotiation from strength' – punishing the Russians by arming the Chinese. But it was also designed to mask disagreement between China and the US on the still unresolved question of US arms supplies to Taiwan, backed up by frequent pro-Taiwan noises from circles close to the President. The target of Mr Haig's arms-bearing gesture was thus ironically the same as its supposed beneficiary. The Americans hoped that by dangling the prospect of their super-modern lethal gadgetry in front of a Chinese leadership bent on modernization, the sting would be drawn from their refusal to fulfil the spirit of the 1972 Shanghai agreement. The arms gambit had already been used in 1978 to buy Chinese acceptance of full diplomatic relations, when President Carter authorized the sale of 'dual-use technology' to the Chinese – such as computers and radars capable of serving a military as well as civil purpose. Then in 1980, after the Soviet invasion of Afghanistan and a visit to the US by Defence Minister Geng Biao, Carter raised the stakes by offering 'non-lethal military equipment' – trucks, cargo planes and helicopters that transport the killers but do not directly dispense death. Though China had not yet ordered a single item of 'non-lethal' equipment, Mr Haig increased the bribe again, provoking a schizophrenic response from China, where there was some disagreement both on how to evaluate the Soviet threat and on whether to take American arms while accepting humiliation over Taiwan.

China and Vietnam
China gave substantial aid to Vietnam in its struggle against the USA, but with the purpose of maintaining the north as an effective buffer zone rather than to bring liberation to the South.

In 1965–6, on the eve of the Cultural Revolution, China quietly made it clear to the USA that it would only intervene directly if America attempted to overthrow the North – just as China had been forced to intervene in Korea when General MacArthur came close to annihilating the North Korean buffer to China's Manchurian border. The internationalist rhetoric which accompanied China's aid, though perhaps genuine at a certain level of Chinese consciousness, was offset by a patronizing attitude which the Vietnamese resented. 'We are fed up with their pompous words and unnecessary advice,' I was told by a Vietnamese official as early as the summer of 1968. He then went on to ask me sarcastically: 'When are the Chinese going to liberate Hongkong?' China imposed tiresome conditions on the passage of Soviet aid to Vietnam on the Chinese railways (they also denied the use of Chinese airspace for Soviet overflights, though this was more understandable). They niggled at Vietnam's offers of peace negotiations with the USA, and the Chinese press ostentatiously ignored several important Vietnamese initiatives during the Cultural Revolution, when for reasons of internal dogma it was impossible to accept that anyone could negotiate anywhere with the imperialists. Yet overall Vietnam did benefit from the 'strategic' guarantee offered by China, since it placed a definite limit upon American expansion, just as China itself in the early 1950s had depended upon the Soviet alliance, in spite of many problems with Stalin, to guarantee the survival of the new People's Republic. This comparison extends to the worsening of relations after the larger socialist ally in each case had finally managed to come to terms with the USA. Once again the USA, unable any longer to resist talking with a communist foe, found compensation in the divisive effect upon other enemies. The origin of the sharp differences between Vietnam and China can be dated very precisely to Nixon's visit to Peking (and soon afterwards to Moscow) which were denounced by Hanoi in scarcely veiled language as superpower manoeuvres at the expense of those waging a war of national liberation. China was accused of 'throwing a life-belt to a drowning pirate', by offering the USA a diplomatic victory to compensate for its defeats in Vietnam, and of setting foot on 'the dark, muddy road of compromise'.

Unfortunately for the Vietnamese, their view was shared by the losing leadership faction led by Lin Biao, who argued that USA–China relations were 'a betrayal of principle, of revolution and of Vietnam'.[24] After Lin's flight and death (two months after Kissinger's first China visit) no Chinese leader could make the same argument and survive.

The end of the war in 1975 gave China a reasonable excuse to cut back its aid to Vietnam. The opportunity for Hanoi to steer a balanced course between the' Soviet Union and China was now sharply diminished, since neither could any longer be accused of 'selling out' a liberation war which had been apparently completed. The death of Zhou Enlai in 1976 removed the last internationalist figure in the Chinese leadership, the man who had protected the flow of aid to Vietnam from the Red Guards during the Cultural Revolution, who had formed a close relationship with Ho Chi Minh during his lifetime and who might conceivably have prevented the ensuing split and war. (Ho's own death in 1969 was followed by the publication of his will in which he appealed, in vain, for an end to the Sino–Soviet split.) As had occurred with Sino–Soviet relations in the early 1960s, potential but containable causes of friction between China and Vietnam – Kampuchea, the border and the ethnic Chinese living in Vietnam – now became focuses of contention once the overall strategic relationship no longer demanded compromise. Discrimination against Vietnam's 'Hoa' population in the North (most of whom still retained Chinese citizenship) had begun to occur, though patchily and without much central direction, after the Nixon visit. The problem was compounded by attempts after liberation to clean up the large Hoa population of mainly urban traders in the South. In spring and summer 1978 more than 160,000 out of the total population in North and South of one and a half million Hoa flooded across the border, anticipating quite correctly that Sino–Vietnamese relations were about to get much worse. China seemed at first to respond with restraint. Then came a high-handed 'demand' in June 1978 that Chinese ships be allowed to evacuate the Hoa from the South, followed inconsistently by closing the border to those who in the North were trying to get across, and soon afterwards by the cessation of all aid.

The land frontier between China and Vietnam had long been clearly agreed, give or take a few local disputes on the exact position of marker stones. But at sea it is a different matter. In 1974 China had already pre-empted the forthcoming Vietnamese victory by 'liberating' the Xisha (Paracel) Islands from the pro-US Saigon forces then in occupation. More recently Vietnam has raised a claim to most of the Bac Bo Gulf (Gulf of Tonkin), perhaps to provide a bargaining counter for any eventual trade-off over the Paracels. Both sides were also well aware of the likely presence of offshore oil in the area. Both populations would now be rallied with chauvinist talk about the sacred nature of their 'sovereign territory'.

Throughout the Vietnam war China had sought to maintain Laos and Kampuchea (Cambodia) as counter-weights to Vietnam, according more publicity to their achievements (and to those of the revolutionary government in the South of Vietnam) than to those of Hanoi. Chance lent a hand when the US-backed Lon Nol coup in Phnom Penh brought Prince Sihanouk and part of the Kampuchean revolutionary left together in Peking to build the Khmer Rouge resistance. What may initially have been a reasonable attempt by China to maintain a regional balance in Indochina led to severe 'tilting' against Vietnam in 1977–8 as the Chinese condoned Pol Pot's brutalities and made no attempt to curb his foolish and adventurist attacks on the Kampuchea–Vietnam border. Chinese leaders in 1979, despite the pretext of Hanoi's own border violations against China, did not conceal that the real purpose of their 'counter-attack' was to 'teach Vietnam a lesson' for having intervened directly in Kampuchea to replace Pol Pot with the pro-Hanoi Heng Samrin regime.

These severe but still local difficulties have been warped almost beyond solution by the larger reality of superpower strategy. Struggling to rebuild a war-shattered country, Vietnam in 1978 found most Western doors closed against it. In the spring Premier Pham Van Dong indicated that it would drop all preconditions for talks to open diplomatic relations with the US, including the demand for reparations. Washington, now fixed on 'normalization' with Peking, voted instead against the Asian Development

Bank being used to channel rehabilitation funds to Vietnam. The tempting terms for foreign investment offered by Hanoi had also borne little fruit, since apart from France most other European countries waited for Washington's approval. Vietnam, which in 1976 had resisted strong Soviet pressure to join Comecon, now did so, and went on to sign a Treaty of Friendship with the opportunistic Russians, who had waited years for this chance to undermine Vietnam's neutral position in the Sino–Soviet dispute. This in turn allowed the Chinese leadership to dismiss the entire Vietnamese leadership as puppets of Soviet social-imperialism, taking a view which exactly replicated the American domino theory of Moscow's expansionist designs.

CHINA'S NEW DOMINO THEORY

... Vietnamese aggression against Kampuchea is by no means an isolated event. This is the Soviet Union's social imperialism manipulating Vietnam, the Cuba of the Far East, to carry out its first expansionist step into south-east Asia: it is part of the global strategic plan of Soviet social imperialism. If we still try to stay submerged in quietism and dream of getting by through appeasement, then today's Kampuchea will be tomorrow's south-east Asia and the other nations of the Asian Pacific region, and yesterday's Czechoslovakia will become the image for tomorrow's Europe and America. If this incident does not arouse enough alertness, if the people of the world do not make the proper preparations of thought, then a new world war will be unavoidable and will come sooner than it otherwise would.

(Vice-Premier Geng Biao, January 1979)[25]

China and the Soviet Union

Just as rapprochement between China and the United States seemed unthinkable until it happened, so it is hard to visualize a bridge being rebuilt in the future between Moscow and Peking after more than twenty years of bitter polemics. Perhaps this very bitterness has created emotional barriers which make a reconciliation more difficult: yet the same could be said of the legacy of twenty years of American containment. In 1971 I spoke to ordinary Chinese citizens who angrily rejected the possibility that Chinese table tennis players – let alone a Vice-Premier of the State Council – would ever visit the United States to reciprocate for the American team which was invited to China in the first act of 'ping-pong diplomacy'. At a banquet for Nixon in Peking, senior People's Liberation Army officers refused to applaud and every-one rejected their gift replicas of the Presidential visiting card! Premier Zhou Enlai went to great pains to explain, in internal party documents, that Nixon's visit was a victory for China and that it demonstrated a 'flexible' application of the Leninist principle that 'we must discreetly and extremely cautiously exploit all the contradictions and weaknesses of the enemy camp' – the enemy consisting of both the US and the USSR.[26]

Are China's nationalistic hostility to the overbearing Soviet neighbour and its new enthusiasm for Western-style moderniz-ation more serious obstacles to eventual reconciliation with Moscow if the power game should require it? In the last years of Mao it could fairly be said that his anti-Soviet obsession inhibited any chance of a compensatory tilt towards Moscow, and for several years after his death this remained a political constraint. In 1969 Mao had told the Russians that the ideological struggle between the two would persist for ten thousand years (later on in a mocking gesture to Premier Kosygin he consented to reduce it to nine thousand years). Chinese officials ever since have maintained that there would be no relenting in the dispute over doctrine, although there could be an improvement in 'state to state relations' if the Russians renounced their expansionist ambitions. In reality the reverse has been true. Since 1978 – when the Deng Xiaoping faction in Peking began to demolish Mao's ideological legacy – the main theoretical positions argued by China since the early 1960s have either been abandoned or quietly shelved. In April 1980 the *People's Daily* announced that the nine Chinese 'commentaries' on Sino–Soviet relations published in 1963–4, written by Mao or by his collaborator Chen Boda (shortly to be tried and sentenced together with the Gang of Four), were incorrect on the nature of Soviet economic policy and its 'revisionist' status. In Chinese academic discussions it was argued that the Soviet Union might still be regarded as a socialist country because the means of production were state-owned. The charge of 'social-imperialism' was now used less often, yielding ground to simple 'hegemonism' – i.e. that the Soviet Union was a large country which wished to dominate others – without reference to its internal class character, which had previously been regarded as crucial to the analysis. At a less formal level, Chinese officials travelling back from Europe through the Soviet Union felt no inhibition about acknowledging that Russian technology and urban development was impressive and that it offered lessons to China.

The question of relations with the Soviet Union has thus been largely restored by Mao's successors to the more pragmatic dimension which it occupied for most of Mao's own life (along with the question of relations with the United States). What threat, actual or potential, does Soviet power present to China, and by what means can this be deterred or offset? Mao's Theory of the Three Worlds, first put forward in 1974 by Vice-Premier Deng Xiaoping, already implied a view of the world based on nothing more subtle than the proposition that the biggest powers were the biggest bad guys. (The 'first' world was occupied exclusively by the US and the USSR; then came the 'second' world of inter-mediate-size capitalist developed countries, e.g. West Germany, Czechoslovakia, Japan, Britain, Canada, followed by the familiar 'third' world of the developing countries.) China's own assertion that it will 'never become a superpower' or adopt 'hegemonist' ambitions follows the same logic: since China intends to join the ranks of the world's most powerful countries, it must consciously forswear the attributes of great power status which it might otherwise acquire.

With the Soviet question no longer enmeshed by ideology – at least at the highest levels of counsel in Peking – it becomes possible to consider coolly the various options available to China, which are now greater than at any time in the past, although still circumscribed by the geo-political reality of the superpowers. This must still be done with great caution for internal political reasons: a 'Maoist' revival would opportunistically seize any evidence of 'pro-Soviet' weakness to fasten the label of 'capitulationism' upon those now in power.

Already in the late 1970s both the Soviet Union and China had in turn tested the water for a rapprochement, although, except briefly, not at the same time. After Mao's death a Soviet moratorium on anti-Chinese propaganda signified Moscow's curiosity, at least, about the intentions of the new Chinese leadership, only to be abandoned when Peking made it clear that 'anti-hegemonism' was still the top priority. It seems likely that the post-Mao leaders were united then in the view that the maximum gains must be extracted from tilting to the US – i.e. that 'normalization' should be completed – before a fresh look was taken at the Russians. Indeed after diplomatic relations were established in February 1979 the Chinese lost little time: the first full Sino–Soviet talks (as distinct from border talks) were opened when Vice-Minister Wang Yuping arrived in Moscow in September to seek 'the solution of outstanding issues and the improvement of relations between the two countries'. The doctrinal explorations mentioned earlier which had the effect of reducing the ideological gap also began to be made public. But this fragile search for some basis of understanding foundered under the inexorable tide which had been set in motion by the events of 1978. The situation in Indochina had already proved a major obstacle to the Moscow talks (China wanted it on the agenda; the Russians refused to discuss the affairs of their Vietnamese ally). Then early in 1980 the view of Soviet hard-liners triumphed and the Russians held their return party – in the streets of Kabul. The talks, already adjourned without agreement except that the next round should be held in Peking, were not resumed.

China and the Bomb

With a new and even more horrendous stage of the arms race threatening us, it is time to look at the attitude towards disarmament of the world's third greatest military power – China. No one has paid much attention to Chinese statements on the subject, and many will assume that Peking's attitude is wholly negative. This is no longer so. China has put forward proposals which, although still couched in very general terms, do address themselves seriously to the problem and should be explored further. With triangular diplomacy now a fact of life, disarmament should be high on the agenda for discussion between China and the US (and hopefully in time to come, China and the USSR) as well as between the US and the USSR. And since China is one of the world's five nuclear powers as well, nuclear disarmament should be at the forefront of the discussions.

How China became a nuclear power is an essential part of the background. The military guarantee offered to China by the Soviet Union – through the Treaty of February 1950 – began to look less credible in the late 1950s. Peking had no intention of sheltering under Moscow's nuclear umbrella. A plan (the details are still obscure) by which the Russians would have supplied nuclear weapons technology to the Chinese broke down. At least by 1958, and probably earlier, China was determined to go it alone. Moscow's quest for detente with the United States, already fiercely criticized by the Chinese, led to the test ban treaty in July 1963. By signing it, the Soviet Union brought the Sino–Soviet dispute finally into the open, for the Chinese – shortly to explode their first atom bomb – could not possibly accede to it. Instead they denounced it, and were denounced in turn as nuclear 'adventurists'.

For many years China had no position on disarmament other than a declaratory one for propaganda purposes. In the 1960s, with relations with both the US and the USSR at a very low point and at a very early stage in China's own nuclear development, there was no serious prospect of negotiations. From the time of the test ban treaty right up until after Mao Zedong's death, the slogan was 'a complete and thorough destruction of nuclear weapons' and no less.

By the mid-1970s the Chinese position on paper had only hardened, reflecting Peking's belief that disarmament proposals were in any case only cynical manoeuvres by the superpowers to mask their own commitment to rearmament. Thus in November 1975 Huang Hua told the UN that China opposed the Soviet idea of calling a disarmament conference on the grounds that this would create 'peace illusions' while the superpowers were moving towards a new world war. China would only support such a conference if all the nuclear powers made a 'no-first-use' pledge (i.e. declaring that each would never be the first to use nuclear weapons in a conflict), and if all the powers withdrew all military forces stationed abroad and dismantled foreign military bases – an obvious negotiating non-starter. A year later Huang told the UN's First Committee that war was inevitable 'some day', and that preparations for defence, not disarmament, were the best ways of delaying it.

Though a slightly more positive note was sounded at the Special Session of the General Assembly in May 1978, the real shift occurred at the first session of the new Disarmament Commission in May 1979, when China put forward a substantially new proposal 'On the elements of a comprehensive programme of disarmament'. This included the following important points:

1. It accepts the principle of proportionate reduction of armaments, both nuclear and conventional, among the major world states including China. Such a reduction must be preceded by a 'drastic reduction' on the part of the US and USSR to 'close the gap' – a proposal which has been made before in the history of postwar disarmament negotiations. It does at least open up the possibility of detailed argument on questions of timing, ratios, strengths, etc., which China has previously regarded as a waste of time. The relevant clause reads as follows: 'When they [the two superpowers] have drastically reduced their nuclear and conventional armaments and closed the huge gap between them and the other nuclear states and militarily significant states, the other nuclear states and militarily significant states should join them in reducing armaments according to reasonable ratios.'

2. It no longer directly opposes the principle of non-proliferation, although it says that this should not be used as a pretext to deprive other countries of the right to develop nuclear energy for peaceful purposes.

3. It clearly distinguishes between the taking of limited steps and the long-term goal of complete disarmament. Under the first heading it proposes the creation of zones of peace (naming southeast Asia, the Indian Ocean and the Mediterranean), and nuclear-

weapon-free zones (naming Latin America, the Middle East, Africa and south Asia).

4. The principle of 'no first use' is no longer insisted upon. (This is perhaps a pity.) Instead all the nuclear powers are asked to make the much easier undertaking not to use or threaten to use nuclear weapons against the nuclear-free and peace zones.

5. It accepts 'strict and effective measures of international control' to ensure the implementation of disarmament agreements, though such measures should not prejudice the sovereignty and security of any state.

6. No preconditions are set for disarmament negotiations, nor do the Chinese proposals suggest – as they have in the past – that such negotiations would be pointless. The Chinese delegate in presenting these proposals did not describe world war as 'inevitable' though saying quite reasonably that 'we are soberly aware that the danger of world war still exists'.[27]

The new Chinese position was repeated, in the same terms as outlined above, by Peking's delegate to the Geneva Disarmament Conference on 5 February 1980. Vice Foreign Minister Zhang Wenjin also stressed that in the Chinese view 'equal importance' should be given to conventional disarmament and nuclear disarmament. He reaffirmed the Chinese statement that 'at no time and in no circumstances would China be the first to use nuclear weapons'. In addition he said that China supports the conclusion of 'an international convention to guarantee the security of the non-nuclear states'. Similar statements were made to the 1981 Disarmament Conference, while in November 1980 the Chinese leadership had finally discarded the doctrine of the inevitability of world war, when the Communist Party Secretary-General Hu Yaobang told the Spanish Communist Party leader Sr Carrillo that in China's view 'it is possible to postpone or even prevent the outbreak of a great war'.[28]

The future
China, and the world, could only benefit by a genuine relaxation of tension between Moscow and Peking – but on condition that

it is not presented as a threat to US–China relations. To tilt in the opposite direction from that adopted at present would merely duplicate the present dangerous imbalance with a different superpower line-up. China should be seeking, if not a state of perfect balance between the US and the USSR, at least some degree of equivalence in its relations with both, and it is in the long-term interests of both powers not just to acquiesce but to encourage such a development. It should by now be abundantly clear that serious regional problems such as Afghanistan, Kampuchea and the Sino–Soviet border are parcelled up in the larger package of superpower relations, and that only the chief actors can unfasten the knot.

A credible solution could begin with the following elements: an increase in Sino–Soviet trade; a drastic scaling-down of the Soviet military presence in the Soviet Far East and the Mongolian People's Republic; Chinese willingness to sign a non-aggression pact as already proposed by Moscow. Such moves are inhibited at present only by a lack of political will and mistrust of each other's motives. Even the first (an increase in trade) would be sufficient to signal to the rest of Asia that readjustment was on the way: local solutions to local conflicts would then be allowed to emerge. But the danger remains that even the most carefully calibrated gestures to ease Sino–Soviet tension will cause panic and fury in Washington where it will be concluded that for the second time this century the United States has 'lost' China. This is why the argument being made here – that a genuine triangularity of great power relations must be based upon a reasonable measure of balance – needs to be reiterated and developed, above all in Washington, but also in Peking and Moscow. A useful start can be made among the allies of both power blocs, whose own relations with China should not be circumscribed by the unspoken vetoes of their American or Soviet big brothers, and who should also make it clear to Peking that peace and disarmament are as important topics for discussion as trade and defence have been up till now.

Conclusion

John Gittings and
Jonathan Steele

'We are living in a pre-war and not a postwar world'

> (Eugene Rostow, Director, US Arms
> Control and Disarmament Agency)[1]

In the 1980s the superpowers are back on centre stage with a vengeance, like two gangs of thugs who, having been put away for a number of years, have now re-emerged to terrorize the neighbourhood by their mutual brawling. Those who are by-standers find it hard to predict the outcome, but they know that they will suffer to a greater or lesser degree. On the worst hypothesis, there will be a final showdown in which all those who have not managed to move to a safe distance (which today means the other end of the world) will be destroyed. The best that can be hoped for is that there will be a temporary relief from this prospect, if the chiefs can get together and make a new pact without some trigger-happy bodyguard ruining the whole thing first. As of autumn 1981, the issue on which there is likely to be either compromise or crisis appears to be that of 'Theatre Nuclear Weapons' in Europe – to be decided by bi-lateral US–Soviet negotiations without the participation of any of the European countries on whose territories these weapons are stationed.

But this is not the only knife-edge scenario which we face in the 1980s. In the Middle East the death of President Sadat – himself the creature of a hitherto quite successful ploy by the US superpower to exclude Soviet influence from the area – has reopened the game, with both sides now tempted to raise their stakes. Crisis could also re-emerge in the Far East, which at the time of writing seems safely in the wings. Yet the emerging superpower force of China, though much weaker than the United States and the Soviet Union, could overnight create new tensions. A decision in Peking to realign in the direction of the Soviet Union would have an immensely unsettling effect unless handled with great sensitivity. Conversely, a decision to intensify confrontation with the Soviet Union by increasing pressure on Vietnam would have the same effect. In addition the problems in southern Africa, so far relatively well insulated from the superpowers by the sheer distances involved, will become more entangled in their affairs, for two reasons. First, because both the US and the Soviet Union are developing new capabilities for long-range intervention, and second, because the very survival of white South Africa must sooner or later become an immediate question as the cycle of repression and resistance develops further. This is in addition to the closer prospects of crisis over Namibia and/or Angola.

It was not only 'detente' which lulled public opinion to forget about the bomb in the 1970s; it was the apparent shift in the centre of gravity of world affairs away from the superpower conflict to the problems and possibilities of the Third World. The cold war was out of vogue; the north–south conflict was in. The 1970s was not only the Decade of Detente but of Development, when the Third World, which had intervened so ineffectively in the traditional balance of power politics of the fifties and sixties through the non-aligned movement, seemed to be mobilizing so much more effectively on the economic front. With the Organization of Petroleum Exporting Countries (OPEC) in the vanguard, the actual or former have-not nations now made their voices heard through the Group of 77 and UNCTAD, and through various short-lived schemes for regional free-trade zones and single commodity producer groups. A mixture of compassion and self-interest fuelled quite a considerable response in the West, spurred by the first oil crisis of 1973–4. The decade was neatly bracketed by the reports of the Pearson and Brandt Commissions, both of which argued strongly that if the industrial West has to export to survive, then it must ensure the survival of those in the developing Third World to whom the exports are directed. Hunger and not the bomb was now the common target. Radical critics of the superpowers also shifted their targets.

With the victory of the Vietnamese against the US-backed regime in South Vietnam it was tempting to believe that the forces of emerging nationalism/revolution/liberation would indeed triumph over the old world – that in the words of Mao Zedong 'men were superior to weapons'. As for the state socialist or 'communist' world itself, the Soviet thaw of the 1960s had lost its promise. But in Vietnam, Angola, China (until Mao died) and even briefly in such odd new phenomena as post-fascist Portugal and post-imperial Ethiopia, some were able to find comfort for the depressing picture in Eastern Europe and the Soviet Union. Euro-communism of the mid-1970s, embracing Spain and Italy as well as (briefly) France, also provided encouragement for the view that the superpower blocs were beginning to break up as the ruling ideologies of both were rejected or transformed.

These visions have faded in a very short time and the realities of superpower politics again fill our front pages. Although in this book we have described both the US and the Soviet Union as superpowers (and China as half a superpower) we do not intend by the use of this term to exclude the important differences between them or to suggest that each is equally dangerous to world peace and stability. Nor are the differences simply the consequence of the disparities in size and military capability. Of the three, we regard the United States as by far the most dangerous. It is the United States which consistently claims the right to world leadership and which, by its denial of parity to the other ranking superpower, has precipitated the current and most acute phase of cold war in the 1980s. It is the United States, not the Soviet Union, which defines its own economic prosperity in terms which demand unimpeded access to the markets of the rest of the world. And if power is the yardstick of ambition, then by all significant economic and military indices, and taking into account Washington's allies and client states, it is still the most powerful nation in the world. The Soviet Union has an extremely unpleasant and repressive system at home, and it defines its security in such a way as to dominate and distort the governments and societies of Eastern Europe. But it does not possess the same economic interest in world empire, formal or informal, as the United States, nor can one foresee the day when it will have the capability to project its power in the same way, far less to capture the multi-nationals, the World Bank, and all the other instruments by which the United States most effectively and least noticeably exercises its hegemony. The threat from the Soviet Union lies in the clumsy and rigid nature of its response to the pressure of cold war competition in which, we should remind ourselves, Moscow has been the weaker adversary ever since it began after 1945. The danger lies mostly in Soviet over-reaction to this situation in ways which may be provocative to its more powerful adversary.

The uncertainty surrounding the future development of China, both in terms of global outlook and of economic growth, must make us hesitate to make any final judgement today about its superpower potential. For what it is worth every Chinese leader from Mao Zedong onwards is on record as insisting that China will 'never become a superpower' – and that if this should after all happen the Chinese people should rise up and protest. On more solid ground, we may note that the generally inward-looking nature of China's historical concerns remains a powerful factor, and that she has not yet carried out any sustained intervention across her borders. We must however also note the declared intention of the present leadership to 'catch up' with the two superpowers in all areas including that of military capability, while we may doubt how this can be achieved.

Nevertheless there is a sense in which all these powers do more than simply translate the behaviour of smaller nation states on to a larger and more dangerous scale, and do have a great deal in common. The element of competition between them is itself a unifying bond which distances them from the ambitions and capabilities of the other powers. Each of the three shares with the other the same two convictions: (1) that its world view is the right one for the rest of the world, and that it will eventually prevail; (2) that it either is or seeks to become one of the world's greatest powers – preferably the greatest. Just as the economies of scale lead to more efficient production, so it may be that the economies of size lead to a more dangerous potential on the part of the very largest countries for action which threatens the rest of the world community. It is in these terms that we are still entitled to talk of the superpower threat as being qualitatively different from the various threats offered by relatively smaller powers at a regional or local level.

Faced with this situation, those countries most closely involved need above all to put some distance between themselves and the policies of the superpowers, thereby weakening the latter's accumulated strength in terms both of actual power at their disposal and of the licence which they presently enjoy to negotiate and to dispute over the heads of their supposed allies. What is called for is a process of 'distancing', the nature of which will necessarily vary according to the particular circumstances of each country. The danger which this policy would represent to superpower interests can be gauged by the speed and ferocity with which their leaders react to any hint that it might be carried out. Popular calls for neutralism in the West, or merely for a reduction in defence spending or at least for restraint in the deployment of new nuclear weapons systems, are quickly labelled as subversive and a challenge to the authority of the state. Attempts by the Polish working class to distance Poland from the Soviet Union are promptly condemned as anti-Soviet. Vietnam incurs Chinese wrath precisely because it continued after the war with the US to distance itself from Peking by maintaining relations with Moscow. The same concerted campaign in the West to discredit the assertion of national independence which successfully undermined the image of Third World neutralism in the 1950s is now being launched again against public opinion which seeks to do the same in the metropolitan countries.

For Britain, a sustained attempt to distance ourselves from the United States should begin with some hard questions being asked about the nature of the alliance and the benefits and losses which it brings. We need to dispel the ideas – which so inhibit serious discussion – that we must be eternally grateful to the United States for its help in postwar reconstruction, or that our shared language creates a unique bond, or that our shared past before 1776 has anything to do with present realities, in short that there are any special reasons why we should have a 'special relationship'. What are the advantages which the alliance brings? What penalties do we incur by the constraints which it imposes upon our economic and foreign policies? Would British interests be better served by a more limited relationship in which successive British governments no longer sought to maintain the pretence that our voice somehow counts for more than those of other nations in Washington? Should Britain not regain the right to oppose firmly and unequivocally those US policies which threaten our interests and those of world peace, without it being regarded as unnatural to do so?

To consider realistically the options which may be available to us, we should encourage public discussion about the ways in which neutral countries such as Sweden, Austria and Switzerland have managed to survive without superpower restrictions being imposed upon their domestic choice of government. It should not be an article of faith either to stay in NATO or to leave it, but a matter for rational debate. Britain should try to prevent the needless widening of the alliance now being attempted by the US. There is no reason why Spain should be rushed into the alliance, and American efforts to blur the edge of NATO so that its effective domain seeps out to cover the South Atlantic and the Persian Gulf should be strongly opposed. The ultimate aim is to narrow the domain of the military alliances, not to widen them. Britain should not hesitate to lobby actively for the adoption of minority viewpoints advocated by other members of NATO – such as the proposal for a nuclear-free zone in northern Europe – instead of being inhibited by the fear of offending the Americans.

On the actual substance of the Anglo-American relationship, the British public is entitled to have access to full information about the agreements which have been signed and the crucial understandings which have been reached, for the most part in complete secrecy. For a start we need to know exactly on what terms a vast network of military facilities in Britain is provided to US forces, before we can calculate what costs these entail in financial and political terms. We might quite reasonably conclude that, at the least, exact inventories of the nuclear and non-nuclear stocks and services held in these bases should be made publicly available with complete dual turn-key facilities affording joint British control over all military movement from them. Such a demand would do no more than to assert the equal rights which have always been claimed for the Atlantic alliance – or to expose the unequal reality which lies behind the claim. We may well conclude after this kind of searching inquiry that steps should be taken to assert our sovereignty and right to independent decision-making even though such measures will not be at all popular in Washington. We shall also want to calculate the economic consequences of 'distancing' ourselves from the dominant superpower in our lives. We may consider too the possibilities of acting in concert with other medium or smaller powers which seek greater freedom of action from the superpowers. All of this is not only a proper subject for inquiry; but as the threat of the superpower conflict grows in the 1980s it has become a matter of vital urgency. The moral conviction with which millions in Europe now seek to reject the cold war must be underpinned by practical argument on the ways and means of doing so. We know already that the argument will be conducted against a hostile background of official propaganda and denunciation, but if we are to survive the 1980s it has to begin now.

Notes

Introduction: What the Superpowers Say

1. Winston Lord, in House of Representatives Committee on International Relations, *Hearings on US – Soviet Union – China*, Washington, USGPO, 1976, p. 168.

2. Airforce General David Jones, *Guardian*, 30 January 1980.

3. *Daily Telegraph*, 11 February 1981.

4. George Ball, in *International Herald Tribune*, 9 July 1981.

5. *Newsweek*, 16 March 1981.

6. General Yepishev in *The Lie of a Soviet War Threat*, Moscow, 1980, p. 97.

7. *Far Eastern Affairs* (Moscow), February 1981, p. 20.

8. Kenneth A. Myers, ed., *NATO: The Next Thirty Years*, Croom Helm, 1980, p. 436 (Haig); p. 4 (Kissinger); p. 55 (Dimitri Simes).

9. *Foreign Affairs Committee, Fifth Report, 1980* (HC 745), FCO memorandum, 20 February 1980.

10. *Daily Telegraph*, 2 March 1981.

The United States: From Greece to El Salvador

1. Michael T. Klare, 'The Traders and the Prussians', *Seven Days*, 28 March 1977. The Traders are a power bloc of more internationally minded merchant capitalists, writes Klare. They include the executives of the large multinationals and international banks. Their position is generally expressed by the Trilateral Commission set up by David Rockefeller in recent years. The Prussians represent an alliance of 'Pentagon leaders, arms producers, right-wing politicos, intelligence operatives, and some domestic capitalists', together with 'a fair sprinkling of cold-war intellectuals' such as Paul Nitze and Eugene Rostow.

2. Lawrence Shoup and William Minter, *Imperial Brain Trust*, New York, Monthly Review Press, 1977.

3. Interview in the *Miami Herald*, 24 August 1980, reprinted in *Central America Update*, Toronto, October 1980. See article by Clifford Krauss in *The Nation*, 14 March 1981.

4. John Lewis Gaddis, *The United States and the Origins of the Cold War*, New York, Columbia University Press, 1972, p. 350.

5. *New York Times*, 23 March 1947. Cited by Richard Barnet, *Intervention and Revolution*, New York, World Publishing, 1968, p. 114.

6. Arnold Toynbee, Introduction to *Survey of International Affairs, 1947–48*, Oxford, OUP, 1952, p. 7. At the time Toynbee accepted that the US had to fill the 'vacuum' left by British withdrawal from Greece, though he did not blame Moscow for the cold war, seeing it as a vicious circle bred from 'mutual suspicion'. But later on Toynbee no longer regarded the superpowers' threat as equally balanced, and wrote that to the greater part of mankind 'America now looks like the most dangerous country in the world' and had become 'the world's nightmare' ('A dire view of the United States from abroad', *The New York Times*, 10 May 1970).

7. Dean Acheson, *Present at the Creation*, London, Hamish Hamilton, 1970, p. 219.

8. These events are described in Lawrence S. Wittner, 'The Truman Doctrine and the Defense of Freedom', *Diplomatic History*, IV, Spring 1980. This study is largely based on US government documents and the official compilation *Foreign Relations of the United States*.

9. Eisenhower's 'Address to the American People on the need for mutual security in waging the peace', *The Pentagon Papers*, vol. 1, Boston, Beacon Press, 1971, pp. 614–16.

10. Joyce and Gabriel Kolko, *The Limits of Power*, New York, Harper & Row, 1972.

11. NSC 68 was first published in the *Naval War College Review*, XXVII, May–June 1975. It is reprinted in Thomas H. Etzold and John Lewis Gaddis, *Containment: Documents on American Policy and Strategy, 1945–1950*, New York, Columbia University Press, 1978.

12. Quoted with other examples in Richard B. Duboff and Edward S. Herman, 'The new economics: handmaiden of inspired truth', *Review of Radical Political Economics*, August 1972.

13. Wilbur Crane Eveland, *Ropes of Sand*, Boston, Norton, 1980.

14. The Laotian crisis is described in Jonathan Mirsky and Stephen E. Stonefield, 'The United States in Laos, 1945–1962', in E. Friedman and M. Selden, eds., *America's Asia*, New York, Pantheon, 1971, pp. 298-305.

15. For example, an article by Fred C. Bergsten in *Foreign Affairs* (January 1972) said that Nixon had 'violated the letter and the spirit of the reigning international law in both the monetary and trade fields', and accused him of encouraging 'a disastrous isolationist trend'.

16. Arthur M. Schlesinger, article reprinted from *Wall Street Journal* in *Boston Globe*, 13 March 1977.

The Soviet Union: What Happened to Detente?

1. Leonid Brezhnev, *Report of the Communist Party of the Soviet Union Central Committee to the 25th Congress*, Novosti Press Agency, 1976, p. 28.

2. Henry Kissinger, *The White House Years*, Weidenfeld & Nicolson and Michael Joseph, 1979, p. 83.

3. Kissinger, op. cit., p. 84.

4. Leonid Brezhnev, op. cit., p. 27.

5. Leonid Brezhnev, *Report of the Communist Party of the Soviet Union Central Committee to the 24th Congress*, Novosti Press Agency, 1971, p. 35.

6. *Istoria Vneshnei Politiki SSSR*, vol. 2 (edited by Khvostov), Moscow, 1971, p. 480.

7. *International Herald Tribune*, 31 January 1981.

8. Kissinger, op. cit., p. 128.

9. Kissinger, op. cit., p. 1141.

10. *Pravda*, 15 September 1957.

11. Brezhnev, op. cit., 1976, p. 33.

12. Letter sent by Richard Nixon on 4 February 1969 to Secretary of State

William Rogers, Defense Secretary Melvin Laird and Central Intelligence Agency Director Richard Helms, quoted in Kissinger, op. cit., pp. 135–6.

13. *Soviet News*, published by Press Department of the Soviet Embassy in London, 22 April 1980, p. 131.

14. *New Republic*, 19 July 1981.

15. Yuri Krasin, 'The international and the national in the revolutionary process', in *New Times*, 7, 1981.

China: Half a Superpower

1. George Orwell, *Nineteen Eighty-Four*, Penguin Books, 1954, pp. 147–8.

2. The Empress Dowager was disastrously encouraged by the successful rebuff of Italy to conclude that China could now 'defeat the enemy', i.e. defy all the imperialist powers. In this mood she and her ministers supported the Boxer Uprising which brought about China's greatest humiliation. See Immanuel Hsu, *The Rise of Modern China*, London, OUP, 1975, pp. 470–71.

3. I have discussed Mao's theory of semi-colonialism in chapter 2 of *The World and China 1922–1972*, London, Eyre-Methuen, 1974.

4. ibid., chapter 7.

5. Henry Kissinger, *The White House Years*, London, Weidenfeld & Nicolson and Michael Joseph, 1979, p. 783.

6. Washington's aim, in a policy passed by the National Security Council in early 1949, was to encourage a Chinese 'Yugoslavia' in which Peking would at least 'be as unfriendly to Russia as to the US' (C. L. Sulzberger, New York Times News Service, in *Hongkong Standard*, 21 July 1968).

7. Every year another twelve million Chinese were born, Khrushchev told Chancellor Adenauer of West Germany in September 1954, and what was going to come of it all? 'We could solve these problems; but it is very difficult. Therefore I ask you to help us. Help us to cope with Red China!' *Erinnerungen 1953–55*, 1966, pp. 527–8.

8. House of Representatives Committee on International Relations, *Hearings on US – Soviet Union – China*, Washington, 1976, p. 65.

9. *The White House Years*, p. 685.

10. Chinese armed forces briefing on the current situation, published in March–April 1973 for internal circulation by the Kunming Military Region, translated in *Issues and Studies*, Taibei, June 1974, pp. 103–6.

11. Quotations from *The White House Years*: (1) pp. 165, 836; (2) 712; (3) 886; (4) 1046, 1052, 691; (5) 194; (6) 1142.

12. *The New York Times*, 14 February 1976, p..22, quoting a letter written by Reagan in 1972 to a conservative supporter.

13. AP–Dow Jones in the *Guardian*, 13 February 1973.

14. K. C. Li, ed., *American Diplomacy in the Far East, 1942–43*, vol. v, New York, 1943, p. 689.

15. Interview of 13 March 1945, *Foreign Relations of the United States: China, 1945*, Washington, USGPO, 1969, pp. 272–8.

16. Speech to National Council on US–China Trade, 4 June 1980.

17. Professor of Politics and Defence Studies, University of Edinburgh, 19 March 1980, evidence to House of Commons Foreign Affairs Committee (HC 745), pp. 45–6.

18. Michel Oksenberg, 'China policy for the 1980s', *Foreign Affairs*, Winter 1980–81, p. 317.

19. Richard Solomon, 'Thinking through the China problem', *Foreign Affairs*, January 1978, p. 324.

20. *The New York Times*, 25 June 1978.

21. *The New York Times*, 10 June 1978.

22. 'Vietnam provoked an attack, says Minister', *Guardian*, 20 February 1979.

23. *International Herald Tribune*, 28 December 1978.

24. Zhou Enlai, December 1971 Report, *Chinese Law and Government*, Spring 1977, p. 85.

25. *Inside China Mainland*, Taibei, January 1981, p. 7.

26. December 1971 Report.

27. *Beijing Review*, No. 22, 1 June 1979.

28. New China News Agency, Peking, 25 November 1980.

Conclusion

1. Quoted in Jeremy Campbell, '120 seconds from doomsday', *Standard* (London), 14 October 1981.

Index